MW01006931

A FIFTH OF TEQUILA

An Althea Rose Novel

TRICIA O'MALLEY

Lovewrite Publishing

A Fifth of Tequila

"Fame gives you everything you've never wanted."

– Ava Gardner

Chapter One

I'VE NEVER WANTED to be famous. I'm happy to leave that particular joy to my mother, the incomparable psychic to the stars, Abigail Rose. With fame comes a level of responsibility and attention to personal detail that I'm just not interested in maintaining.

As evidenced by my best friend, Beau, sighing and handing me a napkin over the smooth wood top of the bar he owned.

"Mustard," Beau said, pointing to where a splotch of yellow had dripped onto my pretty blue sundress.

"Damn it, I just bought this dress," I muttered as I dipped my napkin in my water and worked at the stain.

"Just be glad the paparazzi hasn't fully started harassing you yet," Beau said as he slapped a copy of one of the smutty gossip magazines on the bar in front of me. I secretly loved gossip magazines and devoured them each week when they were delivered to my mailbox every Thursday.

"What is this trash?" I asked, feigning indifference as I unsuccessfully tried to dry the now-grapefruit-sized stain on my breast, making me look like I was lactating.

"Oh please – don't even pull that with me, darling. I'm well aware of how much you love your stories," Beau drawled, throwing up his fingers to do air quotes before picking up his clipboard to continue inventory. It was Monday, the one night a week that Lucky's Tiki Bar was closed, and I was Beau's only company as he tallied inventory and prepped for the week ahead. I was enjoying some us time for once. It had been what seemed like ages since we'd spent any time together – not that I was upset with him about it. Beau was in the throes of readying to open his high-end seafood restaurant on the other end of the strip, while also still overseeing the ever-popular Lucky's.

"I suppose I glance at them on occasion," I murmured, peering at the copy of *Celeb Weekly* and noting the date. How had Beau gotten this week's copy so early? I'd have to contact my subscription service.

Then I spied the cover image and almost dropped the rest of my chicken wing down my cleavage.

"You've got to be kidding me," I exclaimed.

"I most certainly wish I was," Beau drawled, poking his head over the bar, amusement dancing across his surfer good looks. More than one woman had been charmed by Beau's handsome face, easy-going manner, and quiet confidence. It usually took either a strong gaydar or a few days spent in his presence before many women picked up on the fact that he didn't bat for their team.

And what a loss it was for the female population, I mused, as I stared at Miss Elva's image beaming back at me from the cover of the glossy magazine. She was posed on my porch – recognizable by my cheerfully painted shutters and my Boston terrier's pointed ears poking over the windowsill. Miss Elva was wearing her now sold-out trucker hat with *I Heart Miss Elva* emblazoned across the front, and a shockingly pink caftan. I was certain her pirate ghost, Rafe, was hovering by her shoulder, though the camera wouldn't have been able to pick him up.

Only a few of us with extra-special abilities could see him anyway.

"Well, she looks good. Pink is a great color for her skin tone," I said, picking up my mojito for a cooling minty sip.

"You've clearly not read the headline," Beau drawled and I choked on a piece of mint as the words registered.

Tequila Key: Psychic Central of the USA? Miss Elva, Althea Rose, and Luna Lavelle Compete for Reigning Queen of the Underworld.

"I'm going to murder her. I swear to god – the fame has gone to her head," I almost shrieked, picking up my phone immediately to text Luna.

Luna's reply was short: *I heard.*

Meet me at Lucky's.

I tried Miss Elva but, as seemed to be the usual for her these days, her phone went straight to voicemail.

"I could put a spell on her, you know. I'm getting better with my magick. Luna's been training me," I said to Beau and he rolled his eyes, shaking his head before he hefted a box into the kitchen, and on my plea, plugged my now-dead phone into a charger before using his broad shoulders to easily push the swinging door open.

"Psychic Central? What is this nonsense," I muttered, paging through the magazine.

I wondered if that made me a hypocrite. I'm Althea Rose and I co-own the Luna Rose Potions & Tarot Shop in sleepy Tequila Key.

And it looked like we'd just been outed to the world.

Chapter Two

TEQUILA KEY WASN'T EXACTLY unknown to those who were in touch with the psychic world – my mother, of course, being one of their most world-famous citizens. Aside from her notoriety, there wasn't much exciting to be said about sleepy Tequila Key.

Okay, that was a lie. The past six months had seen a significant uptick in the crazies and yahoos wandering our way, and, of course, somehow I'd been pulled into the middle of most of the recent dramas. But, from the outside, our town was your typical small island – one of the forgotten Florida Keys, nothing but a bump in the road along the highway.

A not-so-bright mayor of years past had at some point decided to erect a sign off the side of the highway that sliced through the Keys. It proclaimed, "Tequila Makes It Better," ensuring that tourists pulled over for a picture, but most never ventured much further than that. I had no problem with this, as business was steady for me and I much preferred not having to wait in line for a coffee or to order a mojito. I enjoyed the pace of our small town, the mix of old and new, and knowing that – for the most part – I was allowed to be exactly who I was: a psychic tarot card reader with a recently discovered touch of magickal ability.

I was content with my life just as it was, and the last thing I needed or wanted was to have my name splashed across the cover of a gossip magazine. Though, secretly, a small part of me might have been thrilled at seeing my name on the cover. Not that I was going to admit it.

"Miss Elva has lost her damn mind," Luna said without preamble, as she sailed through the door of Lucky's, her white sheath dress shimmering with threads of silver. At this point I was convinced that Luna just wore white to be smug; she knew it was virtually impossible for me to keep white clothes clean. She refused to give me any magick spell that might help in that department, so I was left wearing darker colors that would hide my tendency to attract dirt and stains. I slid a glance down to where the splotch on my chest was slowly drying. "Love the hair," Luna said, sliding into the stool next to mine.

I'd recently switched out my hot pink streaks for a teal color – feeling more in touch with the sea lately, I suppose. I had a tendency to change up my hair color as often as my moods shifted, which was frequent. Beau had made no comment on my hair, which meant he preferred the pink, but was kind enough to refrain from offering his opinion.

I wished I had his restraint.

"That's exactly what I said. She's clearly gone off the deep end." I flipped the copy of the magazine open and paged through all the pictures of Celebrities Being Normal as they artfully posed while getting an ice cream cone or walking their dogs.

Beau handed Luna a gin and soda water with a slice of cucumber before leaning over to buzz her cheek with a kiss. We all bent over the magazine as I found the main story.

The silence stretched out as I worked to form words.

"At least it's your cute bathing suit," Luna finally said, patting me lightly on the shoulder.

The headline screamed a bold question in large black font: *Psychics or Frauds?* And the reporter had chosen three pictures of us – Luna looking like a million dollars in a wide-legged pale blue jumpsuit with a sassy gold belt wrapped around her waist, Miss Elva in a sparkling caftan and a turban that shone like a disco ball, and me...

Bending over on the dive boat to pull my wetsuit off, my ass all but bared to the world.

As every woman knows, bending over in a bikini can be touch-and-go at best, and even more so when you're wearing a thin one that fits comfortably under a wetsuit. Also, wetsuits can be particularly tricky to tug off, so this image had me balancing on one leg, tugging at my wetsuit, with all my bits and pieces wobbling about for the world to see.

In full high-definition resolution.

Groaning, I buried my face in my hands. I knew I wasn't the skinniest girl in the world and for the most part, I embraced my curves. But couldn't this reporter have tried for a modicum of decency in portraying each of us fairly? Or at the very least fully-clothed? I had professional images on my website she could have used, I thought, glaring at the name on the byline.

"Thanks a bunch, Noelle Hardy," I grumbled.

"Tequila Key has become a hotbed of psychic activity," Luna read, still gently patting my arm to calm me down. "When the international spotlight hit this little town a month ago with the Chadwick Harrington case, attention was drawn to a new fan-favorite, Miss Elva, a renowned voodoo priestess. As fascination about Miss Elva grew, more was revealed about this so-called sleepy little town and the insidious psychic services that are being pandered to locals and tourists alike."

"Pandered," I sputtered, almost ripping the magazine in two in my rage.

"The world-renowned psychic to the stars, Abigail Rose – even more famous than Miss Elva – is from Tequila Key, having first started her business there and then passing it on to her daughter, Althea. Who knew that psychics could transfer their power like that? This reporter has been sent to investigate. Stay tuned for our six-part series into the seedy underbelly of the psychic dealings in Tequila Key and tell us whether you think they should move forward with a new psychic-themed reality show. What do you think – are psychics real? Visit us on Facebook and vote yes or no in the comments or follow us on Facebook to track our investigation in Tequila Key."

"Six-part investigation? Who does she think she is? CNN? NPR?" I grumbled, slurping my mojito down to the last drop and leaning back to cross my arms over my chest.

"It's just a puff-piece," Luna said. "Obviously they're

looking for something to sensationalize, and they're capitalizing on the attention Miss Elva's getting."

"Did they say Bravo was going to do a reality show down here?" Beau perked up as he slid me my second and final drink along with my now semi-charged phone. I rarely drank more than two cocktails – first, because I didn't like to cloud my head when I was doing readings for clients the next day, and second, because being a psychic requires you to always have your wits about you. It takes an incredible amount of energy to block people's thoughts and to tune out visions that pop seemingly endlessly into your brain. Alcohol pulls those strongly built walls down. Three drinks was my absolute max, but I usually stuck with one or two if I was going to indulge.

"That they did," Luna said.

Beau beamed. "I hope that means Andy Cohen will come down here. I just love him." He was almost gushing now, and I shot him a glare.

"What? He's a doll." He shrugged.

"This is not about your celebrity crushes. This is about the fact that they are trying to tear apart our business and our reputations," I said, slamming my fist into my palm, the rage still simmering low in my belly. "And the fact that this twat of a reporter can't seem to take a professional photo."

Immediately contrite, both Beau and Luna patted me, assuring me that the picture really wasn't as bad as it looked.

I'd powered my phone up, and now it beeped with incoming text messages.

I think you look healthy – from my mother.

You do not need to lose weight – from my father.

I've got a new line of swimming suits for fuller-figured girls – from one of the boutique owners downtown.

Don't let them get to you. Our profession has been under attack for ages – my mother once again.

Do you think you'll be on a reality TV show? – from my cousin.

I like when you bend over – from Trace. That sent a blush across my cheeks and I chuckled, sending him a kissy-face emoji back. Trace and I were… in a fairly good place, all things considered. And there was a lot of considering to be done in that department, I thought, as I smiled at his cheeky response to my text.

Are you okay? – from Cash. Which made me pause and glance at Luna.

"Cash? Have you heard from him recently?" Luna asked, taking a small sip of her drink as she surveyed me over the rim of her glass.

"Not since he found out that Trace and I were hanging out." I shrugged; my emotions were a tangled mess when it came to the men in my life. One was the perfect boyfriend on paper – but unrelenting in his expectations of a girlfriend. The other was one of my best friends, and there was a constant worry of losing him if I allowed a serious romantic relationship to take over our friendship. It was a delicate dance, and one that I wasn't entirely sure I was up to negotiating.

"Ugh, look at this," Beau complained, sliding his phone over to us. On it was Theodore Whittier's Facebook page – or should I say, the platform where he liked to spew conservative nonsense about politics and how the rich folk in the gated community of Port Atticus frowned on the likes of us lowly street urchins who had lived in Tequila Key for ages. Theodore Whittier's family liked to pretend they were the founding family of this town and acted as such whenever possible.

"It's time to run these frauds out of town. They've been bringing danger to our small community for years, and keeping tourism out. This just goes to show how awful these psychics are. We need to pass an ordinance to put them out of business." Theodore Whittier's post continued on for several paragraphs in that same vein.

My eyes got huge in my face. I reminded myself to use my inside voice and made myself take a few deep breaths before speaking.

"I'm going to kill him," I said, using my inside voice, which made it sound even creepier.

"The man seems to have a short memory when it comes to the number of times you've saved him or helped this community," Luna said as she gestured with her glass, her feathers finally ruffled.

"I told you this was bad news," I said glumly, tapping the magazine. "You know what this is, don't you?"

"What?" Beau asked.

"This, my friends, is a good old-fashioned witch hunt."

Chapter Three

I'D FINALLY HEARD from Miss Elva last night, after she ignored several of my increasingly heated text messages.

Calm down, child. Any press is good press. Just think how your business will flourish!

That had been her one and only text, and I'd almost thrown my phone at the wall. Had it not been for Trace yanking the phone from my hand and distracting me with a much more pleasant diversion, I'd probably have a shattered screen on my new iPhone today.

I smiled over the rim of my coffee cup at him, cheerful despite my annoyance with Miss Elva and the fact that she was happily sharing the gossip magazine and the images contained therein on all her social media.

"I've got a dive group coming in at eight," Trace said, draining his cup and dutifully putting it in the sink. He looked every inch the sexy dive instructor today, with his blond hair tied back with a leather cord, a long-sleeved black t-shirt with the PADI symbol on it, and his bag of camera gear slung over his shoulder.

"I'm kind of bummed we haven't been diving in a few weeks," I admitted, bending to toss the moose toy that Hank had dropped at my feet.

"Well, someone has to be all super popular and overly booked up these days, doesn't she?" Trace said, tugging on a strand of my teal hair before making his way to the door.

"I know, I know," I grumbled. I followed him across my main floor to the kitchen. I'd knocked down walls and opened up the first floor to become one large kitchen, dining, and living area when I'd first purchased the house. "But I've been out of the shop so much of late that I wanted to at least get some of my regular clientele back in rotation. Plus, it's good for me to consistently practice my skills."

"I understand. We still get to spend time together, so I'm not complaining. I'd just prefer it if you'd try to, you know, keep yourself safe on the job as best you can? I know it seems like a lot to ask what with the type of work you deal in, but I do worry about you." Trace's smile only heightened his sexiness as he grabbed me for a hot kiss before saying goodbye to Hank.

I closed the door behind him and sighed. He was right – I'd had more than my fair share of trouble in the last six months, so I couldn't blame him for wanting to ensure my safety.

"The men in my life are always so worried about me," I said down to Hank. His little butt wriggled in delight as I bent to pick up the toy and launch it across the room, and he went scrambling after it in sheer joy. Sometimes I wished my life could be as simple as my dog's.

I checked the clock and decided there was time for one

more cup of coffee before I had to leave for my first reading at the shop.

Thinking about the men in my life had me flashing back to Cash's text from the night before. My feelings were still all tangled up when it came to him. Though I was happy to be… whatever it was I was doing with Trace – I refused to allow him to call me his girlfriend – I would be lying to myself if I said I didn't think about Cash sometimes. On the surface, Cash was a dream partner – he was financially secure, drop-dead gorgeous, and had a good heart – but he also had some hang-ups with his family and certain expectations when it came to the type of woman he envisioned himself with. And let's be honest here – a tattooed psychic with teal hair didn't exactly fit into his charity dinners, fundraisers, and investor vacation lifestyle.

Which was fine, ultimately; we'd given it a go and it hadn't worked. But I was still exploring my feelings for Trace and figuring out the shift from friend to lover, all while working past any residual feelings for Cash. All in all, I sometimes had moments where I considered swearing off men altogether and getting myself a ghost companion like Miss Elva's pirate, Rafe.

Not that he made life any easier, come to think of it.

A soggy toy landed on my foot, and I smiled down at a beaming Hank.

"You're the only man in my life worth my undying love, Hank," I said, and Hank danced in circles around my feet, his black and white body writhing in ecstasy when I scratched above his cute little bum.

So what if I was a few steps away from being a crazy dog lady? Animals are one of the best things about life, in my opinion. I didn't trust people who didn't like pets – cats *or* dogs, though secretly I was far more a dog person than a cat one. Not that I was judging.

My not-so-deep thoughts about men and life as a potential spinster followed me on my bike ride into work. I preferred to bike on my beach cruiser to work, waving to my neighbors, and watching the town wake up before the heat of midday rolled in. You'd be surprised how active a small town in a hot climate can be in the early hours of the morning. There was a reason the siesta was invented – namely because nobody wanted to work in the midday heat that crept through the Keys, blanketing it in humidity, unless the winds were kicking up that day.

And I'm not saying I'm proud of it, but I almost – *almost* – turned my bike right around and left Luna to fend for herself when I saw the crowd of reporters camped outside the Luna Rose Potions & Tarot Shop.

Almost.

Until their eyes landed on me.

Chapter Four

IT WOULD BE dramatic to say that pandemonium broke out when the press saw me, but who was I kidding? I secretly loved drama.

It was a madhouse.

Flashbulbs popped in my eyes and I suddenly understood why all the celebrities wore sunglasses in their photos. It was quite disorienting to have all those lights flashing, like a strobe ball at a seventies disco club.

Throwing my arms over my face, I pushed past two camera guys along with a reporter or two and rushed into the store, panting from the exertion of pushing through the crowd.

Did I mention that I was a bit dramatic?

Luna eyed me from where she stood just inside the door, arms crossed over a linen sheath the color of oatmeal, with a stunning turquoise statement necklace stealing the show. A pair of slim blue clips pulled her blonde hair back in a column from a face clear of makeup and eyes that danced with amusement at my entrance.

"It really wasn't that difficult to make it into the shop," Luna pointed out.

"Let me have my moment," I insisted, fanning my face and glaring angrily through the window at the reporters who still lingered there, clearly bored. They were most likely wondering why their bosses had even sent them on this assignment – though I'm sure the promise of sunshine and margaritas had made it easy for them to accept the gig.

"Should I start calling you Miss Elva then? This town can only handle so many divas," Luna drawled as she wandered back through her side of the shop, all elegance and grace, while I took a moment to compose myself.

"Nope, we're good. Miss Elva can hold that title. I wouldn't be able to compete with her for it anyway. For that matter, I'd need to get a hold of her to even try and compete," I muttered, stopping to admire a particularly fetching display of seaweed soaps and face masks artfully arranged in a bowl of gold-tinged seashells. "These are pretty – new logo?"

The masks bore a white and gold label with a lotus flower instead of the pentagram Luna typically used.

"Pentagrams freak people out. At least that's what I'm finding. For those who don't really understand their uses, it just says something dark, like 'devil' or 'evil.' And since I create and infuse my products with love and light magick, I figured I'd go with something pretty like a lotus."

"It is pretty. A hibiscus or bird of paradise could be pretty as well, for other items," I agreed. I glanced up at where the reporters still ranged outside on the front porch. "Why are they not coming inside?"

"I suppose it must feel safer outside." Luna shrugged a shoulder delicately and sniffed, carefully slitting open an envelope with a gold letter opener.

I always admired that she used a letter opener. It seemed so much more adult than what I did – which was to rip open the envelope and typically mangle whatever mail was inside of it in the process.

"You did magick, didn't you?" I asked gleefully. Luna shrugged again, a hint of a smile on her face.

We both looked up when the bells chimed at the front door, and I saw that it was my first client of the day – a regular who needed consistent guidance in her life. She looked particularly rattled by the reporters lingering out front.

"Sorry, Shelly. I know it's annoying," I said immediately.

"You'd better not give up my regular appointment if you're going to be all famous now," Shelly sniffed, tugging at the strap of her purse as her eyes darted around the shop.

I muffled a sigh and pasted my customer service smile on for Shelly, and waved her over to the screen that separated the two parts of the little cottage that housed the Luna Rose Potions & Tarot Shop.

"I believe in rewarding loyalty, Shelly. I'd never give up one of my favorite client's standing appointments." I smiled.

"Good, because I'm feeling extra nervous about a visit from my husband's family in a few weeks. I'm certain my mother-in-law is trying to kill me."

My eyes met Luna's over Shelly's head as I ushered

her into my part of the store. She made a circular motion with her finger by her head to indicate she thought Shelly might be crazy, and I stifled a laugh. If I refused service to all the clients I thought might be a little crazy, I'd be out of a job.

Plus, after the things I'd seen and done in my life, crazy wasn't exactly a word I wanted to examine too closely – in case I saw my picture sitting next to the definition in the dictionary.

Stepping into my shop from Luna's was a shock to the senses – like going from a yoga studio to an eighties Jazzercise class. Where Luna's side was all soothing, elegant tones and prettily packaged goods, mine was an explosion of velvets and colors and leopard prints. Glass shelves lined the walls, covered with hundreds of oddities and antiquities relating to my craft that I'd picked up over the years. In the corner, Herman, my plastic skeleton, sported a new vintage t-shirt I'd pulled from a resale shop. It proclaimed his love for chicken and waffles.

"Now, why do you think your mother-in-law wants to kill you?"

"Because she texted me and said she could kill me for not inviting Brant's sister along as well when they come. But we don't have space!"

And so began my appointment. It was something I was used to at this point, and I let my client chatter while I set up my tarot cards and went through some of my own mental rituals that would allow me to clear my mind and focus on giving her the best reading I could, for whatever was bothering her at the moment. I flipped on some music – instrumental reggae – to drown out the increasingly loud reporters outside and began the reading.

"Okay, Shelly, let's see what we can find out about your mother-in-law," I said, instructing her to cut the deck of cards and shuffle them, thinking about what questions she wanted answered, and to let the cards absorb her energy. I did my best to stay focused on the task at hand, but it was still annoying me that reporters were clamoring around my place of business. I know they say that all press is good press, but not if it interfered with my work or stopped clients from wanting to visit the store.

By the end of the reading, we'd determined that while Shelly was certainly not a favorite of her mother-in-law's, she'd likely be relatively safe from harm at the woman's hands – though Shelly sniffed and insisted she was going to make sure her mother-in-law took a bite of all the meals she served first. I couldn't argue with her logic – one can never be too cautious, I suppose.

I waved goodbye to her as she left through the rarely used side door in my shop. The door, once opened, always let in a burst of sunlight that left me momentarily blinded, which was how I found myself blinking at two men standing in front of me, who had seemingly appeared from nowhere.

"Althea Rose, I presume?" The taller one, with a closely shaved head and a tailored suit, looked around my shop with barely concealed disdain.

"You presume correctly," I said, my eyes scanning over him and then his companion, who looked like a smaller version of the man, aside from the fact that he was wearing a velvet bowtie in brilliant purple. Mini-me glared across the room at me and I glared right back.

"Ah, well, this answers everything I need to know," the man said, scanning my office once more with his cold brown eyes before assessing me – clearly not liking what he saw.

"I think I'll be the judge of what you need to know. What exactly is the question you're wanting an answer for?" I said, dismissing Mini-me and focusing back on the taller man. He was handsome, I'd give him that, and I could see where ladies might find him appealing, if they went for the slick-suit-and-asshole vibe. Which was most women at some point in their lives, if my informal studies of human character were right.

"I wanted to see what the competition for my services in this little town is. And, well…" The man held out his hand to gesture toward Herman, and sniffed in disdain once more. "As you can see, it isn't much."

Dropping my shields, I let myself scan the energy of both men and was surprised – and, despite myself, intrigued – to find that they each held their own unique blend of power.

"So you're a psychic," I said. I leaned back to cross my arms over my chest and then let my eyes drift lazily to Mini-me. "And you're his minion, who's just playing with the psychic realm."

I was delighted to see I'd hit the right spot, because Mini-me's head looked like it was about to explode. All color drained from his face and his fists clenched at his sides, and he began to wheeze a little, like the steam just beginning to escape a kettle on the boil.

"Murray, if you could step outside, please, and consult with the reporter. Let them know where we've decided to set up shop."

Mini-me – or Murray, that is – shot me a death glare before stomping from the room and slamming the door behind him. I blinked to let my eyes adjust to the change in light, and raised an eyebrow at the man who still stood across from me.

"Murray's got an anger issue," I said, reaching out to sweep the tarot layout in front of me into a pile. I began shuffling the cards to clear Shelly's nervous energy from them before I read for my next client. Speaking of which, I glanced at my wristwatch to see they'd be arriving momentarily.

"He's a hothead, but fiercely devoted and while, no, his powers are not as strong as mine, I do find him useful." The man shrugged as if to say, Assistants; what can you do with them?

"And you would be?" I asked, meeting his eyes as I shuffled.

"Ah, yes, my apologies. I'm Dominick St. Germain. I'm here to show Tequila Key – and the world, really – what an actual psychic who takes their business and their craft seriously looks like. It's going to be a real delight to show the world that this profession can have some integrity and actual use – versus whatever it is you're playing at in here."

So here's the thing: I don't always have the best control over my temper. But we were in my shop, with a client about to enter the door and reporters on the doorstep – and attempting one of my newly-learned magick spells would most likely be more disastrous for me than it would be for this Dominick character. So, for once in my life, I played it cool.

"You certainly know how to charm the ladies, Dominick," I said coolly, and was rewarded with a flash of a smile in his handsome face. "But coming into my place of business and insulting my integrity as a professional, as well as blatantly informing me you're looking to steal my clientele, seems very... childish to me," I continued. I was even happier to see a glint of anger cross his face. The man did have his ego, I decided.

"I would call it direct, not childish," Dominick said, rocking back on his heels and steepling his fingers together as he regarded me.

"Nah, seems much more like schoolyard bullying tactics. Or an attempt at intimidation. Luckily, I'm smarter and more powerful than you." I secretly delighted in seeing that flash of anger on his face again. "I've read your energy and can see where you are lacking. However," I said, holding up a finger to stop him when he was about to speak, "because I'm a smart entrepreneur, I welcome competition. There's more than enough business in this town for the both of us and I wish you the best in your little endeavor, whatever that may be."

There, see? I can be an adult.

Dominick quirked a smile at me and turned to go, pausing once more – for dramatic effect, I'm sure – by the door.

"We'll see if you feel the same once you've spoken with the producer and see the money on the table. Only one of us can be a star, Althea. And by the looks of you and your little shop, you have no chance of giving the people what they need. That's just fine – you will serve as an excellent contrast for those who want to see what type of psychic they shouldn't waste their money on."

The door clicked shut behind him before I could throw something at his big bald head, and I forced myself to breathe. His laughter floated back to me as he entertained the reporters on the front porch. I forced my temper down, working hard to clear my energy before my client, when the rest of what he'd said registered with me.

What producer?

Chapter Five

IT WAS my last client of the day who informed me, with much delight, about the major gossip in town. I'd yet to even have a chance to speak with Luna about the visit from this Dominick character, as we'd both been slammed all day. It was increasingly annoying to me that Miss Elva had been right once again: Our shop sales had skyrocketed and my schedule was booked full for weeks in a matter of hours after the magazine had hit. I'd had to block off some free time on my calendar or I'd be booked clear through for six months.

"Can you believe they want to make a reality series about the psychics in Tequila Key? They say there's a high level of paranormal activity here too," Erin, a gossipy but harmless stay-at-home mom, gushed to me as she rushed in late to her appointment. "It's so exciting! You could be on Bravo or something. I guess it depends what station they sell the show to. Or is that how it works? Gosh, I just love Bravo. I could watch the Real Housewives shows all day. They're all so glamorous. Do you think they'd make a

Real Housewives down here?" Erin slapped her hands to her face in delight, then fear crept across her face.

"I don't think…" I began, but she cut me off as she sat and dropped her Coach tote bag on the floor.

"I'd need to get my hair dyed, and perhaps a new wardrobe. I have gotten a little relaxed with the whole stay-at-home mom thing. You don't see all those women running around in yoga pants and a t-shirt stained with baby spit all day." Erin laughed nervously and twisted her rings, her pretty face scrunched in concern.

"Those women have a staff of nannies and hair stylists, Erin," I said gently, bringing her back to reality. "They can afford to look like a million dollars because they sell their image as their currency. It's an investment for them – just the same as being as dramatic as possible so that the cameras keep rolling."

"Do you think that's what you'll do, then? Like, summon spirits and have séances?" Erin asked, leaning over the table to study me with a critical eye. "Your hair is okay because wacky colors are expected for psychics, but perhaps you should go more extravagant with your outfit and accessories."

Miffed, I looked down at what I'd thought of as one of my prettier maxi dresses – a deep eggplant color with red floral stitching on the hem and at the bust – which I'd accessorized only with one long amethyst pendant on an intricate gold chain.

"What's wrong with my dress?"

"It's fine, I suppose. But I'd add a lot more necklaces, maybe some big earrings, rings on every finger." Erin scrutinized me critically. "The tattoos are cool, so that works in your favor, but what about some darker eye makeup? You'll want your face to pop on screen."

"There is nothing wrong with my eye makeup, Erin. It's daylight out. I can't go around with raccoon eyes all day, I just…" I held up a hand to stop the direction of this conversation. "Can you tell me what you're talking about, please? I'm completely out of the loop."

"Oh my god, didn't you hear?" Erin gasped and held her fingers to her mouth dramatically. "They're going to make a reality show about psychics. They're down here scouting which psychic they want to be the star. I guess it's going to be huge – there's apparently been a huge uptick in the nation's interest in all things psychic and paranormal. They're even going to maybe bring like ghosthunters down here to measure paranormal activity. Do you think there are ghosts here?" Erin shivered in delight.

My mind immediately flashed to Rafe, Miss Elva's pirate ghost, and how he annoyed me on the regular. I suppose the world would be shocked and entertained by the likes of Rafe, but to me he was largely an annoyance.

"Of course there are ghosts, Erin. You wouldn't be here to try and talk to a dead loved one if you didn't think spirit energy carried on into the afterlife, right?" I pointed out gently. Erin had booked me for a mediumship appointment in which she hoped to reach her grandmother who had passed on.

"No, I suppose not. I think sometimes I may look at the spirits or souls of loved ones who've passed on differently than ghosts floating around. I guess the word 'ghost' means more of a haunting in my mind," Erin mused.

My eyes flashed to my watch to check the time. Her

appointment time was rapidly dwindling away, and it was the end of a long day for me.

"While that is certainly fascinating news about the potential reality show, I can tell you I have no interest in being famous," I said, and pointed to the clock. "But I do have an interest in making sure you get your questions answered. What will you be asking your grandmother today?"

"Is it because of the bad picture of you in the magazine?" Erin asked, bulldozing me with her honest concern. "I understand it wasn't flattering, but you'll have time to lose weight before they start shooting the show."

I bit my lip and stared silently at the ceiling, counting to ten before looking at Erin and smiling brightly.

"Great, I'll keep that in mind. Now *about your grandmother*," I bit out.

"Oh, right, right. I've been trying to find a locket of hers for ages. I wanted to save it for my daughter and I lost it years ago. It's been bothering me," Erin said, and we got down to business.

Thirty minutes later, I'd given her the location of the locket and gladly closed my door after reminding her that her babysitter could only stay until five. As she rushed out in a panic, I sagged against my door and surveyed my shop.

So what if it was chaotic? I liked the unusual odds and ends I'd acquired over the years. If truth be told, much of it was for show – but there were times where bits and pieces were used in a spell or came in handy for a ritual. I thought I hit the right notes of unusual and charming in my décor – not kitschy or fake. Annoyed with myself for letting a jerk like Dominick put doubts in my head about my business, I poked my head through the screen to see Luna ushering the last lingering shopper toward the door.

"Good luck with the crystals, Marybeth. I'm sure they'll clear the energy and bring more creativity to your office," Luna called after her, then blew out a breath, tucking a loose hair or two behind her ear. For Luna, that was positively rumpled.

"Did you hear –" I began, but Luna cut me off.

"About the reality show? Yup, and that little twit Murray tried to threaten me about stealing the thunder from his majestic boss, Dominick. Guy's got a real zealous crush going on there."

"For sure – some hero worship, or something of that nature. Definitely thinks he's as good a psychic as his master, that's for sure."

"Do you really think they're trying to do a reality show down here?" Luna asked. "How would they even have heard about us?"

Our eyes met across the room.

"Miss Elva."

Chapter Six

"WHO IS THIS MONSTER?" Luna demanded as soon as we'd met at Miss Elva's house. Well, I should say a few blocks from Miss Elva's house, because getting closer to where she was holding court on her front porch was proving to be difficult, what with the throng of reporters and people clamoring for her attention.

"I don't like it one bit," I muttered, elbowing my way past a man carrying a heavy camera on his shoulder.

"The trucker hats were one thing – I thought they were cute. But what's happened to our Miss Elva? The one we know and love? It's like she's turning into a dramatized version of herself," Luna hissed as we worked our way to the foot of the stairs to Miss Elva's porch.

"Fame's gone to her head," I agreed, and stopped to look up at where Miss Elva fielded questions, an agitated Rafe at her side.

"She looks good though," Luna said.

I had to agree. I didn't know anyone else who could pull off her ensemble: a brilliant orange trucker cap with

Miss Elva's slogan on it, a deep blue caftan with silver sparkles on the trim, and earrings that dripped past her shoulders. It should have been ridiculous, and yet on Miss Elva? It worked.

Damn that woman for always pulling it off.

"I would look like a mental patient if I wore that," I grumbled, throwing an elbow into the ribcage of a reporter who crowded me.

"Ow," he complained, and then his eyes lit as they landed on me. "Hey... aren't you Althea Rose?"

"Nope, that's my sister," I lied, and made a move to step past him.

"Althea Rose doesn't have a sister." A woman, her girl-next-door look undone by a lethally sharp smile and a wicked intellect in her eyes, stepped forward and sized me up. "My name's Cate London and I'd like to interview you for a chance to star in our show."

So this must be the producer, I thought, and sized her up. She had a delicate build and a face that was just vaguely familiar, and I surmised she'd worked her way up from reporting to producing – most likely fighting tooth and nail the whole way, judging by the way she refused to budge from in front of me.

"No thanks," I said, making a move to step around her. "I'm all set on that front."

"I don't think you understand, Miss Rose," Cate said, stopping me once again with her body, all while the cameraman blatantly filmed us.

"What I understand is that you're blocking my freedom of passage," I said, nodding to where she refused to let me step onto the porch stairs.

"My apologies," Cate said, immediately easing back. "I understand my passion and determination can often be mistaken for something else."

My eyes caught Luna's, and we both said "Bitch" in our heads.

"But I am very enthusiastic about my job. And this really is an amazing opportunity. I'd at least like the chance to discuss the details with you, so that you understand exactly what you're turning down."

I had to hand it to her – Cate London was a smart woman. She knew when to press and when to back off, as well as when to dangle a tidbit that could pique interest. Taking my silence for assent, she handed me a card from the trim pocketbook she carried.

"I'll meet you at Lucky's Tiki Bar – tonight at eight? My treat. I understand your friend owns the restaurant and it seems like just the spot for a great burger and a beer."

Oh yeah, she was smooth, I thought, buttering me up with compliments on Beau's restaurant. Because judging from her trim figure, I suspected she rarely ate and when she did, burgers certainly weren't on the menu for her. Deciding that I'd let someone else pay for my dinner – and that I'd make sure to watch this woman squirm while she was forced to eat for once – I nodded at her and then held up my hand to indicate she should move.

"Great, great. And, oh, your friend Luna – yes, what a face for the cameras. She's not psychic though, right? But maybe something else? Hmm, I think she'd be a great secondary character – kind of like a supporting role. Yes, the fans would kill for her cheekbones alone – hell, so would I. Oh yes, and add in Miss Elva? This could be a dream show," Cate said, speaking as though Luna wasn't standing right in front of her. The look Luna shot Cate mirrored those killer cheekbones of hers and I bit back a more strongly-worded retort.

"She's a person, is what she is," I said, snagging Luna's arm and pulling her past Cate. "And she's standing right in front of you as you speak about her. Perhaps you'll want to work on your tact if you expect us to even remotely consider anything you're offering us, because I can tell you as of now – it's a hard no."

"I'm sorry," Cate said immediately, tucking a wisp of hair back and smiling sheepishly. "I have a bad habit of doing that – speaking out loud when I see stories shaping up in my head. I really think you'd both be amazing on a reality show, however. But I'd like to present you with full details at dinner tonight instead of in the midst of this." Cate whirled her finger in the air at the crowd around us.

My eyes landed on Murray, Dominick's little mini-me, who had shouldered his way close enough to hear what Cate had said and was currently glaring at us like we'd stolen the show from his master... er, boss. Two little red spots of rage hovered on his cheeks as he tried to contain himself while he got Cate's attention.

"Miss London, I spoke with you earlier. The name is Murray – I'd been telling you about Dominick? One of the greatest psychics that's ever lived? Unlike... well, you know – the hacks in this town." Murray's eyes flitted over me as he drew Cate to his side.

"Oh, right, right. I was going to call you. I'm not entirely sure Dominick is a fit for what we're looking for," Cate began, but Murray cut her off.

"I think you'd be surprised at what we have to say. Really, really surprised. You might feel… compelled to think otherwise and consider us for your show once you've seen what power Dominick possesses," Murray said, handing Cate a small card. I'd already begun my way up the steps so I couldn't hear the rest of what was said as Murray drew Cate away from the crowd, and frankly, I didn't care. I had bigger things to worry about than a competing psychic who wanted to be on a reality show that I had no interest in being involved with.

"It's about time you wenches showed up. I expected you to be here earlier trying to steal Miss Elva's thunder. Now it's gotten so crazy, because – well, just look at how amazing my love mountain is." Rafe smiled at where Miss Elva posed and preened. "But now I could use you for the distraction. Getting her to take a break from her adoring public is nearly impossible. I'm sure if you ladies do something to distract them I can get her inside for a moment to rest."

I briefly wondered what she needed to rest from – standing on her porch and waving at people?

"How do you suggest we distract them, Rafe?" Luna murmured quietly, facing away from the crowd. It was tough to remember not to speak directly to the pirate ghost when he hovered in front of us; Luna and I could both see him clear as day, but those on the sidewalks couldn't.

I looked over my shoulder to where Murray glared at us from across the street, standing by a small SUV that Cate London was currently getting into. A prickle of unease hit me as he stared us down, and I wondered if he could see Rafe.

"You could take your clothes off," Rafe was saying, gesturing to Luna. "You've got a lovely body. This one, though... well, the boobs are good."

"I swear to the goddess, Rafe, I will send you back through the veil," I threatened, storming past him and unceremoniously grabbing Miss Elva's arm. "You, inside, now. You've got some explaining to do."

"I think Althea needs more sex. A well-sexed woman isn't this angry," Rafe said, and I just shook my head as I dragged Miss Elva into her house.

One of these days Rafe was going to get what was coming to him.

Chapter Seven

"I DON'T THINK lack of sex is the issue, Rafe," Luna said as we settled into Miss Elva's living room. The room itself was a favorite of mine – a mix of Restoration Hardware meets gypsy wanderer.

"I understand it makes a woman cranky," Rafe said, floating across the room to study my face, his hat at a rakish angle on his head.

"Do you know what else makes women cranky? Telling them they are constantly cranky," I pointed out.

"Well, if you weren't constantly cranky, I wouldn't have to point it out, now, would I?" Rafe parried.

I looked at the ceiling and counted to ten. I was doing that a lot today, which just went to show what type of week I was having.

"It's not the lack of loving in my life that makes me cranky, so much as the ghosts who are constantly annoying me," I said to Rafe, and he looked around suspiciously.

"What ghosts?"

"You, Rafe. You are a pain in the ass."

"How can I be a pain in the ass? I'm not even in your ass. I don't understand this meaning," Rafe said, and I was once again reminded that he was an actual pirate from centuries ago, and plundering the high seas and having his way with any women he wanted was the norm for him. This whole "women's rights" thing was still a big learning curve for Rafe.

"Now, now, Rafe, you know you need to go easy on her. She stresses easy," Miss Elva said. She was perched on a low-slung love seat, the folds of her caftan draping softly over her, and she managed to look like a queen holding court.

"I do not stress easily. It's you guys. You all make me crazy," I grumbled, plopping into a seat to glare across at Miss Elva and Rafe.

"She in a snit about that picture in the magazine?" Miss Elva asked Luna.

Luna smiled before sitting and delicately crossing her legs. "Well, I mean, they could have picked a better shot. I think, had it been a picture of you in that position, you'd be a little miffed as well," she said gently, smoothing her dress with a perfectly-manicured hand.

"Why would I be upset about that?" Miss Elva wondered.

I blinked at her and glanced at Luna, who gave just the smallest shake of her head. Even though Miss Elva was a large woman, she bore no hint of insecurity, and carried her considerable mass with complete confidence.

Which was a constant reminder to me that I needed to be happy with and embrace my body just as it was, I thought, because nothing stopped Miss Elva from wearing what she wanted, being who she was, or having a slew of admiring men who were more than willing to be a part of her life if she allowed them to do so.

"It's just that everyone else had a less indiscreet photo and, well..." I paused, as there was nothing I could say that wouldn't make me sound whiny or insecure, so I waved it away. "The point is – just what exactly are you doing?"

"Doing? Child, I'm just here living my best life. What are you doing?"

"Luna and I are dodging reporters on our porch, fielding offers of reality TV shows, and dealing with competition now, that's what – all while you seem to just hang out and preen on the porch," I said, actually surprised at the tone of my voice. It was the closest I'd ever come to being angry with Miss Elva, and even she raised an eyebrow at me. She leaned back and gave me a long hard look.

"If you can't handle having a famous friend then perhaps we need some space in our friendship," Miss Elva said, honestly shocking the crap out of me. It was so unlike her that I wasn't even sure how to respond for a moment.

"It's not that we aren't happy for your fame," Luna interjected quickly, attempting to soothe any ruffled feathers. "It's just that all this new attention has caused some difficulties for your friends, is all. And it seems like you aren't quite acting the same – you've been a bit more..." Luna made a little humming noise as she tried to come up with a word to describe Miss Elva's recent behavior and her lack of support for her friends.

"Self-involved? Selfish? Fame-hungry? Disappearing act of a friend?" I listed off, not caring if I made her angry.

"Says the girl who disappeared for weeks after the Valentine's Day party and her break-up with Cash." Miss Elva glared at me.

"Excuse me if I wasn't all that excited to see this one" – I glared daggers at Rafe – "who had potioned me against my knowledge or will and led me down a path I didn't choose."

"It didn't look like you were complaining when you were wrapped around Trace on the boat," Rafe shot back.

My mouth dropped open. "You were watching?" I screeched.

"Of course. I wanted to see if you would actually have sex for once – thinking it would make you less cranky. Also, you know," Rafe said, gesturing toward my chest, "boobs."

"If you weren't dead, Rafe, I swear I'd kill you all over again," I threatened.

"Seems to me I'm not the only one who's changed," Miss Elva huffed. "You used to like Rafe. And you were much more understanding of your friends when they had successes in their lives. Women should celebrate women, you know."

I opened my mouth but Luna held up a hand to quiet me, and I bit my lip for the gazillionth time that day and stared across the room at the wall.

"It's not that we aren't celebrating you, Miss Elva. We love you and are your friends. It just seems you've been acting a bit out of character lately and we, as your friends, are concerned. On top of it, we aren't that happy with having national exposure – negative exposure, at that – on our businesses. Now we've got reporters down here trying to strong-arm us into a reality show and taking pictures of our every move. It's a bit disconcerting."

"And how was business at that shop of yours today?" Miss Elva asked, her gaze steely and her shoulders stiff.

"It was busy, yes – I understand that exposure can be helpful," Luna began, her gaze bouncing between Miss Elva and me.

"Uh-huh. Child, you aren't complaining about the increased business but you want to come down on me for being the one who brought it to your doorstep. Mmm-kay. Doesn't make sense, does it now, Rafe?"

"No, it doesn't, my love mountain. But I've always said they're ungrateful wenches."

"That's it. I'm out. Let me know when you come to your senses. Oh, and so help me god, if you sign me up for a reality show without my permission, I'll never speak to you again," I threatened, already across the room and at the door.

"Psh, child, you know I'm the one who'd get the reality show, anyway, even if they are kind of looking at you right now," Miss Elva called, and even though we all knew it to be true, it still kind of stung. Which was messed up – I didn't even want to be *on* the damn show, and now here I was thinking I should compete with one of my best friends over it.

"Althea, don't," Luna said.

I just shrugged, but wisely kept my mouth shut. Miss Elva was one of my oldest friends, and sometimes we argued, but it wasn't worth it to me to say something mean.

Once again proving that I could actually be an adult on occasion, I simply walked out onto the porch and continued down the stairs, shouldering my way past the cameras clicking pictures of me until I could swing a leg over my bike and head home.

I had a dog to feed.

Chapter Eight

THE BEST THING about having a dog is that they're always delighted to see you. No complications or expectations for the relationship, other than feeding them regularly and offering them companionship. In return, you get unlimited snuggles and sheer happiness every time you walk through the door. It's hard to stay upset when there's twenty-five pounds of delight wriggling at your feet when you get home.

"Hey, Hank. Did you have a nice day? What did you dream about?"

Hank looked up at me, his pointy ears cocked and his mouth wide and smiling.

"Pizza?! Again? We've got to stop giving you table scraps," I laughed down at him and crossed the room to slide the back door open so he could race across the yard and down to the little slice of man-made beach that I'd paid entirely too much money to have put in. But it was worth every penny to see Hank's delight when he barked at whatever he saw in the water and raced away from the waves that rolled up onto the beach.

I was feeling funky – annoyed and a bit melancholy about having words with Miss Elva – and I wasn't sure I even wanted to go meet this Cate London woman for a late dinner. That's the problem with being psychic: Every time you have a disagreement with someone, the emotions linger for a long time. Being empathic is a huge part of what makes our abilities work, yet at the same time it can be a hindrance when it comes to muddling our way through our own personal emotions and daily interactions.

A splattering of sea water snapped me from my mood. I shrieked and looked down to where a beaming – and soaking wet – Hank had dropped a piece of driftwood at my feet. Clearly delighted with himself, he ran in circles around me until, to Hank's sheer joy, I stooped to pick up the stick and launch it across the yard.

My phone flashed with a text message from Trace reminding me that he was taking a group on a night dive tonight and that I shouldn't expect to see him. I sent him my thanks and a few cute kissy-face emojis. I shied away from using the heart or saying 'love' – it was something we danced around, and I was more than fine with avoiding it for the moment. Not that long ago, Trace had just been one of my best friends, someone I wouldn't have hesitated to refer to as someone I loved.

But 'loving' and being 'in love' were two very different things.

I felt like I still had a lot to learn about being in love. There was no harm in treading carefully right now, I mused as I opened a bottle of wine and poured myself a half glass to carry to the back veranda, where I'd be able to throw the stick for Hank for a while to run off some of his energy.

My phone vibrated again with another text, and I knew without looking that it was from Cash. I closed my eyes for a moment and let my thoughts wander – about how I felt about him and whether I missed him or not. Then I opened my eyes and picked up my phone.

Still not speaking to me? Please know that I just wanted to make sure you were okay after the article. I hope that we can still be friends. Or at least friendly. I'm dating someone as well and I know our paths will cross once in a while on Tequila Key.

He was dating someone? Already? Well that…

I paused and forced myself to take a deep breath. Wasn't that exactly what I was doing? "Double standards, Althea, double standards," I lectured myself.

I typed my reply, then read it out loud: "Sorry I didn't get back to you – had a flood of messages from the article yesterday. I'm obviously not pleased, but will deal with it. And I'm happy to hear you're doing well. Stay in touch." I looked down to where Hank panted at my feet, his head cocked in a question.

"If I tell him to stay in touch does that mean I'm violating some sort of girlfriend code with Trace?"

Hank bounced from paw to paw, so I took that as an agreement and deleted that part of the text.

"There – that was friendly, right?"

Hank seemed to agree as he sat, his tongue lolling out, his eyes never leaving the stick in front of him. I launched the stick for him and answered Luna's incoming call.

"You're going tonight, aren't you?" Luna asked, and I could hear the annoyance in her voice at this entire mess. Luna was one of the calmest and most centered people I knew – she was wildly powerful with her own white magick, loved her store, had a great boyfriend, and was content with her world. Unlike many people, she didn't crave or seek out the limelight, as it wasn't something she needed to feel fulfilled.

"I'm going. If nothing else, just to shut this woman down. I think if we make it clear that we aren't interested in this story and ask her to stop bringing attention our way, perhaps it'll stop. I mean, how long can they stalk our porch before we get Chief Thomas involved?"

Surprisingly, our newest chief of police actually seemed to like Luna and me – so long as we cooperated with his ongoing investigations – and for the most part, let us be. Unlike the last chief, who had tried to murder us.

"What's up with you?" Luna asked, obviously hearing something in the tone of my voice. I quickly detailed the text messages from Cash.

"He's dating already?" Luna said, her voice incredulous.

See? That's what best friends are for.

"Yeah, but technically so am I."

"But Trace was kind of already in the picture. It wasn't like you went out on Tinder and found yourself a brand-new boyfriend in two weeks. You've been friends, with something underlying, for years and years. Totally different situation."

Did I mention that I loved my best friend? We all need someone to validate our crazy once in a while.

"I love you. I'll see you at Lucky's. Let's shut this story down."

Chapter Nine

WHEN I CAUGHT myself fussing with makeup just for grabbing a burger at Lucky's, I knew I was more intrigued about the reality show than I had thought. What was it about potential fame that goes to people's heads?

I promised myself I would be immune to the lure of being famous, thinking darkly of Miss Elva's dramatics, as I parked my car in my spot at Lucky's and waited for Luna to meet me in the mostly-full lot. Pleased that business was good for Beau, even in the off-season, I smiled at Luna.

"Tone the smile down a bit there, killer. You look ready to take a bite out of someone," Luna laughed at me, and I realized just how on edge I was.

"Sorry, I'm annoyed with all this. I'd like for life to settle down into a normal routine for once, and the crazies to let us be," I said, taking in Luna's outfit. "Great jumpsuit."

"Thanks, it's new. I picked it up in Miami on a trip with Mathias," Luna said, holding her arms out to twirl in her casual but chic breezy, mint-colored, sleeveless jumpsuit with a heart-shaped neckline and wide-leg pants. I'd look like a potato with legs in a jumpsuit, but always admired how Luna could pull off virtually any look.

"It's great. I love that color on you, too," I said, and we turned to go inside.

"You're looking nice too – did you do your eyeliner?"

"I stopped myself once I started getting concerned about what I was wearing. What is with this whole thing? I don't even care about being famous because I don't want to deal with the annoyances of that life, but now all of a sudden I'm intrigued."

"I think that's called being human," Luna laughed. We strolled up to the tiki bar, the faint sounds of the expected Jimmy Buffet pouring from the wide-open porch, where tiki torches burned to ward off the ever-encroaching mosquitos.

"Are you immune to all this? Like, do you see yourself being on a show?" I asked as we swung inside and waved to the bartender on duty. Beau wouldn't be here tonight; it was his night off, though I suspected he was probably finalizing things over at his other restaurant. One thing I could say about Beau – the man wasn't lazy.

"Cate's already here." Luna pointed to where the reporter had commandeered a table in the corner, without her ever-ready cameraman present. Smart, I thought. "And, I suppose for a minute it crossed my mind that it would be fun or interesting – but then I considered how much I like my privacy, and it no longer interested me."

We threaded our way through the tables and waved at a few locals we knew. Theodore Whittier steadfastly ignored us from the table where he held court, loudly talking about some zoning something or another that the town council was probably up in arms about this week.

"That's true, you are fiercely private," I agreed.

"Witches typically have to be," Luna murmured, and then we were standing in front of Cate's table. She was typing furiously into her iPhone. It was a full minute before she registered that we had arrived, and I could tell she was flustered by the way she glanced up and then back down at her phone, before coming to a decision in her head and shoving her phone in her purse.

"Are we interrupting something?" I asked, curious despite myself. It wasn't like she hadn't known we were going to be here. She'd invited us, hadn't she?

"No, sorry, just talking with Legal about shutting down a few hangers-on here that are trying to muscle their way onto the show." Cate waved it away, forcing a laugh, but the tension line by her brows didn't ease as she took a sip of her champagne spritzer.

"Dominick and his ever-so-worshipful assistant, Murray?" I asked, sliding into the seat across from her and signaling to Marylou, a waitress who helped during the week.

"Not so worshipful. Seems this Murray character thinks he should be the star of the show," Cate muttered, then snapped her lips closed. "I shouldn't be talking like this. It's unprofessional."

"But you don't like him," I surmised, testing to see if she would explain more. "I didn't either, when they paid me a visit."

Cate's gaze met mine, then danced away as she took

another sip of her drink and eased back in her chair marginally.

"I'm not surprised they visited you. They're sizing up the competition at the moment, though I'd never indicated that I was interested in Dominick for the lead of the show. And the fact that Murray thinks he has more ability or stage presence than Dominick is laughable," Cate bit out.

"I'm surprised by that. I was referring to Murray as 'Mini-me' in my head," I admitted, hoping to keep Cate talking so I could get a better read on her.

"He's an annoying little gnat, and he isn't half the psychic Dominick is. But none of that matters – not for our market, at least." Cate's forehead smoothed out as she put on what I deemed to be her 'I'm trying to get my way' look. "You see, our audience is largely composed of women and they want to see women in the lead roles. It's why the Real Housewives shows are so popular. Women are the ones watching these women – not men. I honestly believe that if we put a few attractive women psychics on television who are able to actually help people and answer some questions about the paranormal, we'll have a huge hit. And you, Luna, and Elva all fit the role perfectly."

"*Miss* Elva," Luna and I automatically corrected.

"My apologies; Miss Elva. It seems she's more than ready for the spotlight, but it's getting you two to agree that will prove to be tricky. So instead of pitching you all the benefits, I'll just ask you straight out – what would it take to get you to be on the show?"

I have to admit, she'd surprised me. I was expecting more of a pitch or a presentation, but she seemed tired and whatever Murray had harassed her with had apparently left her more than a little annoyed. It wasn't a bad approach, in my opinion: Cut the BS and get right to it.

"One million dollars," Luna said smoothly. Cate laughed, the sharp edges of her face smoothing in delight.

"Mojito, vodka martini, and three burgers – medium – with a side of your fried pickles," I ordered when Marylou approached, and glanced at Cate's almost-empty glass. "And more champagne for the fancy one here."

Marylou snorted out a laugh, not needing to write the order down, and worked her way back through the crowd, snagging empty glasses and shouting to regulars as she went.

"I'm not sure I can eat a burger right now," Cate said.

"Oh, you'll just love it. Don't you want to sample the local flavor? Since you might be filming down here soon?" I smiled sweetly at Cate, who proved wise enough to not argue with me on the small things.

"Fine. I'm sure it will be delicious. We will, of course, want to feature your local hang-outs on the show, so I'm certain Lucky's will get a lot of coverage, if this is your main spot. Your friend wouldn't mind that, would he?"

"I assume he'd be delighted, but he isn't exactly struggling." I waved my hand to encompass the bustling room.

"Your business will explode as well. With an audience of around eight to ten million per episode, I'm certain you'll be flooded with business. And that doesn't even begin to cover the endorsement deals, sponsorships, book options…" Cate went on to list all the benefits of starring in a show. I had to admit, it was dizzying.

We paused as Marylou appeared back at our table, one arm carting a tray full of steaming food and our drinks.

She casually plopped our drinks in front of us, followed by our burgers, each one nestled in a funky bamboo basket with fried pickles, three sauces, and coleslaw on the side. The smell alone was enough to make my mouth water. Beau knew how to serve comfort food right – displayed well, the right portions, and just the perfect blend of flavors.

"Wow, this looks delicious," Cate said, despite herself. She picked up a fork and knife and cut off the tiniest slice of burger to nibble on.

"Try the pickles, too," I said, cutting my burger in half and dipping it in a ranch-style sauce before taking a bite. I was hungrier than I'd realized – the long day hadn't left me much time to eat.

"Delicious," Cate decided as she ate half a pickle, and I tried not to sigh. It wouldn't kill this woman to eat a sandwich once in a while.

"What's in this for you? If I may ask?" Luna asked and I looked over at her as she took a healthy bite of her burger. Smart woman, I thought.

"An executive producer spot I've been battling for. It's come down to me versus some cocky jerk who wants to make more real estate shows. Like we don't have enough real estate shows? There's an entire channel devoted to the million different ways you can buy and sell homes," Cate scoffed, eating another pickle in her angst.

"And you think a show on psychics will be just what the network needs?" I asked.

"I think people love this stuff. There's something comforting about believing in the afterlife, that you can communicate with those who have crossed over, and that you might be able to have some control over your future if you just ask a psychic for direction."

"But not you," I said, meeting her eyes.

"No," Cate said, looking me dead on. "I don't believe in any of this. But that doesn't mean I can't produce a great show about it."

"Why don't you believe? Aren't you even curious?" Luna interjected.

"Full disclosure?" Cate asked, leaning back as she sipped her champagne and considered her words. I noticed that her finger tapped the glass erratically, and I wondered what was bothering her.

"Please," Luna said. I kept silent, instead choosing to enjoy my crispy fried pickles with the absolute certainty that I wouldn't have to be on television any time soon.

"I think it's for weak people," Cate said, then held up a hand to pause our responses. "Not the psychics them-selves, or what it is you do. But I think that people who need it for whatever it is in their lives are weak. I think you determine your own future, based on how hard you work, or hard choices you've had to make. Not some pre-destined path or the universe telling you to go a certain direction."

"Not much for the self-help, are you?" I asked, taking a sip of my mojito and leaning back in my chair to stop myself from finishing off my pickles in 2.4 seconds.

"I think those who help themselves don't need it."

"Well, I think I've heard all I need to hear," I said. First of all, I wasn't about to argue with a skeptic, as you rarely changed people's minds, but I also didn't want to be on a show produced by a skeptic either. Who was to say what angle she would take with it all?

"Before you say no, tell me what your reservations are," Cate insisted, a bulldog to the end.

"Why would I hold my profession up to scrutiny like that?" I asked, leaning closer so she could see that I was dead serious. "Especially with a producer who's a skeptic. Skeptics are the worst – they're always seeking to prove people wrong instead of to prove anything right. We already work in a profession that's subject to constant ridicule and derision. It wouldn't make sense for us to expose ourselves and our livelihood to a producer who doesn't even believe in what we do. Your natural inclination isn't going to be to edit this in a flattering way. You'll edit it to be sensational, laughable, or scandalizing – whatever gets the most ratings. And I, for one, don't need or want that kind of energy in my life."

Silence settled over the table and Luna just shrugged, nodding her head in agreement with what I'd said.

"I could certainly work a clause into your contract stipulating that I wouldn't malign your profession –" Cate began, and I held up my hand to stop her.

"Eat your burger," I said gently. Cate looked down to where she was silently tearing the bun to pieces in the basket, but not actually eating the food.

"Oh, well, I'm not that…" Cate said, and I cut her off.

"Eat your burger. Enjoy this great bar. And understand that these are people's lives you're playing with here. I happen to like mine just as it is. And nothing you've offered or explained here has remotely interested me. In fact, it's only solidified my decision not to touch this project with a ten-foot pole." I smiled at her, kindly, because ultimately the woman was just trying to do her job and I couldn't blame her for that.

"I'll follow up with you in the morning to see if you've changed your minds," Cate said as Luna and I both stood in unison.

"Please don't," Luna said, speaking in her firm voice, which I'd seen freeze out more than one person before.

"Sleep on it. This could change your lives forever," Cate called after us.

"That's exactly what I'm afraid of."

Chapter Ten

OF COURSE we couldn't even have our exit from the restaurant be television-worthy, I thought in annoyance as we approached the door, my nod to Marylou signaling for her to put the meal on my running tab. I tipped all the staff out each month when I paid my bill, and everyone who worked there knew I was good for it.

Theodore Whittier, of the Tequila Key founding family Whittiers, hovered by the door, clearly waiting for us. He looked like twenty pounds of sausage stuffed into a ten-pound bag. Perpetually sweaty, always opinionated, and forever in a snit about something, Theodore was one of my least favorite people in town. Not to mention that he tried yearly to run our businesses out of town. Luckily, the rest of the committee was smart enough to not pull business permits for every business in town that Theodore had a personal grudge with, or there would have been few businesses left to support our little tourist economy.

"Theodore," I said, barely containing my grimace. I

crossed my arms over my chest and waited for whatever he was going to spring on us.

"Ladies, always good to see you both," Theodore bit out. I actually laughed out loud, I was that surprised. A red flush swept his face and I knew he was working hard to bite back what he really wanted to say.

"What can we help you with, Theodore?" Luna asked politely, and he nodded at her. He'd always been nicer to her, probably because she was more polite than I was – and shorter. Theodore liked looking down at people, and as a fairly tall woman, he was forced to meet me eye-to-eye.

"While you know that I may not always be the most…" Theodore looked up as he scrambled for a word. "…supportive of your businesses, I am beginning to see how they could benefit the community."

I swear you could have knocked me over with a feather. If I'd had a recorder running, I'd replay that to myself and the whole town for weeks – just to hear Theodore eat crow on repeat.

"That's quite a change in tune from the one you've been singing the last few years. I can't possibly imagine what's making you say this now." I rolled my eyes at Theodore and pushed past him to continue out to the parking lot. I was no longer interested in hearing what anyone else had to say about this stupid reality show. If this was how people were acting and we hadn't even agreed to do it, I could only imagine what would happen if we actually did sign up for the show.

Naturally, Theodore followed us out to the parking lot.

"I don't think you ladies see how much this could benefit our little town. Think of all the exposure to local businesses! Tourism would increase, people would vacation here – we could even put a sign up by the road to get rid of that faded Tequila sign. It would be excellent press."

"Even if they made a laughingstock of us?" I whirled on Theodore, and to his credit, he stepped back.

"Well, you know, they say that any press is good press. I really think this is a win-win for everyone. I think you should at least consider it. Please. For me," Theodore said, backing off with his hands in the air as he crossed to where his ostentatious yellow Hummer was parked. Who needed a Hummer in the flatlands of Tequila Key – and a bright yellow one at that? It wasn't like he was going to get lost. The Key was about twenty miles wide, total.

"Or you could just hand the show over to us and we'll make this town look amazing. It's obvious you're doing nothing for it."

I whirled to see Murray standing behind us, a smirk on his smarmy little face. I wanted to throat-punch him.

"Go for it. Nobody's stopping you from taking the show," I said, narrowing my eyes at him in a glare. I swear, if I never heard another word about this stupid reality show again, it would be too soon.

"It seems the producer thinks women will be better – but she doesn't really understand the nature of our abilities yet." Murray shrugged.

"You seem to think very highly of yourself," I said, smiling at the cocky little jerk. "From my understanding, you're willing to throw your boss under the bus to try and steal the show out from under him. I wonder how he'd feel to learn about your disloyalty?" I let my voice get louder as Dominick slowly approached from the other side of the parking lot.

"What's this about, Murray?" Dominick asked.

"She's trying to steal the show from us," Murray all but shouted, his voice carrying across the parking lot. "Stupid fake psychic said she's better than both of us combined, and that nobody will take the spotlight from her."

"What!" I screeched, fed up beyond reason at this point. "I said no such thing! First of all –"

Luna grabbed my arm and pulled me toward my car. A crowd had formed behind us, which, I belatedly realized, was what Murray had wanted. As flashbulbs went off, he preened for the cameras while Dominick's calculating gaze followed us.

"I'm ready to do the show just to steal the little shit's thunder," I hissed to Luna, who all but shoved me in the car.

"Go home. It's not worth it. We'll just end up in the magazines and this will never end. If we don't give them anything to talk about, eventually they'll see that we're fairly boring and the reporters will leave, and Cate will find another town to film," Luna said gently.

I knew she was right. "Fine," I said, glancing over to where Murray entertained the cameras. "But, can I –"

"No, you do not get to reverse your car over Murray," Luna ordered, reading my mind perfectly.

"Fine," I grumbled.

This 'being an adult' thing was getting pretty old.

Chapter Eleven

AFTER A RESTLESS NIGHT OF SLEEP, one where I dreamt of being crowned prom queen at a high school dance – and let's be clear that I didn't even attend prom – I blinked awake to Hank snoring at my feet. His little smushface of snorts and grumbles comforted me and I reached down to give him a pet, my eyes going to the empty space in bed next to me.

It wasn't that unusual for Trace not to sleep at my place. Some nights he worked late and crashed out just to get up super early for diving the next morning. I was proud of him for how hard he worked, and I knew it was important to him that he run and operate his own business – which meant long hours and excellent customer service.

Plus, I had to admit I liked the alone time once in a while. Could this end up being the perfect arrangement – we dated, but lived separately, and remained individuals who came together for mutual companionship when we were in the mood?

"And wouldn't that just look great on a reality TV

show?" I asked out loud, and Hank stretched, his little puppy legs stiff in the air, before rolling over to tilt his head at me expectantly.

"I know, I know. We aren't doing the TV show. Though Miss Elva is wrong – you'd be the star of the show, buddy," I said to a delighted Hank, who rolled back over for tummy scratches before we both got up to start the day.

The knock on my door while I was feeding Hank should have come as a surprise so early in the morning, but I was getting used to visitors and interruptions at all hours of the day. Dropping my mental shields, I scanned the energy at the door.

"It's just Beau," I told Hank, who had exploded in a cacophony of barking as soon as he'd heard the knock. I suppose when your days were focused on eating and chasing a ball, visitors brought a lot of excitement.

"Hey, handsome," I said, opening the door to an impeccably dressed Beau. I was even more happy to see him when I spied the pastry bag he carried, along with two to-go cups of coffee.

"I come bearing gifts," Beau said with a bright smile, but I noticed the tension lines on his face, and my eyes zeroed in on the magazine tucked under his arm. I grabbed it from him before he could do anything to stop me. "Damn it, Thea, not fair. I have hot coffee in my hands."

"One of which I will take off your hands immediately," I said, snagging a cup and looking at the magazine to see what I'd have to deal with next.

"I was going to ease you into this after you'd had your coffee," Beau grumbled, bending to pet an ecstatic Hank, who immediately raced across the room and came running back with a stuffed snowman to offer Beau.

"Best to just rip the Band-Aid off," I said, and then almost wished I'd waited when I saw the cover.

Battle of the Psychics – Who will be picked to star in Bravo's newest reality show?

This time Dominick had been included in the rotation of photos, much to Murray's delight, I was sure.

"Luna warned me about this. She warned me not to let them get to me," I said, anger beginning to burn low in my stomach as I stabbed my finger into the cover. An exceptionally unflattering photo of me – surprise, I know – from the night before, when I'd yelled at Murray in the parking lot, was emblazoned across the cover. Though I hadn't been exactly screaming, the flash and the photographer's angle made it look as though I was shouting obscenities at Murray, while he looked just as enraged.

"It's an enticing photo," I said, trying my best to disengage. "I'd buy this magazine for sure."

Beau studied my face carefully before taking a sip of his coffee and letting out a little hum of disbelief.

"And how do they even get these magazines printed so quickly? That was what – twelve hours ago? Did you get an advance copy?"

Beau shrugged, a devilish smile flitting across his handsome face.

I narrowed my eyes at him. "I know that look. You're dating someone."

"Well... I wouldn't say dating exactly," Beau said, and I squealed.

"Details. Immediately. How could you have been keeping this from me?"

"Girl, we've barely seen each other for weeks now. And it's not anything major. Just a dalliance, really. He lives in New York. I met him through my publicist for the restaurants when I flew up there last month. We've kind of stayed in touch and since he works in the industry, he sends me magazines here and there – especially if they're concerning anything that has to do with our little town."

"I knew it. Damn it. I knew you had an in for getting the magazines early," I grumbled as we moved to sit on the back porch, where my wide bamboo fans swooped lazily to dispel any bugs that wanted to interrupt our morning coffee. Hank dropped the snowman at my feet and I launched it across the yard absentmindedly as I tried to decide which to focus on first – the new man in Beau's life or the dramatic magazine cover.

Deciding once again to go with the whole 'adult' theme, I focused on my friend.

"Tell me everything. What's his name? What does he do? Do you even talk to Cash's brother anymore?"

Beau had also had a brief liaison with Cash's brother, so when we'd both broken up with our respective members of the family, we'd commiserated over mojitos and unful-filled expectations of those with old money.

Beau stretched, and then crossed muscled arms over his chest, his eyes twinkling as he laughed at me.

"His name is Brad, he's scandalously younger than me, and he will not be breaking my heart in any way, shape, or form. He's hungry to move up the ladder at his PR agency, and has no aspirations of moving to a sleepy little town in Florida. I'm so busy that I don't have the time or inclination for a full-time relationship, so we've found ourselves in a part-time enjoyable open relationship. As for Cash's brother, no, we don't speak. And I'm fine with that, in all honesty. Sometimes it's better to just let things die than to hang on to any lingering wisps of what could have been, you know? Holding onto the thought of what could have been doesn't, in fact, make it a should have been. So, no, we don't speak. What about you? Any word from Cash lately?"

"He messaged me when the first magazine hit the stands to see how I was holding up," I said, picking at a loose thread on my magenta maxi dress. "When I responded, he also let me know that he was dating some-one, and that he hopes we can at the very least be friends when he comes through town."

"Ouch," Beau said, understanding perfectly how that would sting.

I shrugged one shoulder, picking up the toy for Hank and launching it across the yard. As Hank scrambled after it, I blew out a breath and shook my head to shake off the melancholy that had slipped over me.

"I'm doing the same. He has every right to date. And Cash has investment properties and developments here – he's right that we'll see each other. He did the adult thing and addressed it, and I'm certain we can be friendly when we see each other."

There, that sounded mature, no?

"And still…" Beau trailed off and looked at me. "Ouch."

"Yeah." I blew out a breath and wrapped a teal curl around my finger. "Hypocritical though it may be... ouch."

"We'll always have each other, honey." Beau patted my leg and I smiled at him, glad he'd come over to see me – even at seven o'clock in the morning.

"Don't I know it. And Luna and Miss Elva..."

I frowned down at the cover and reached into the pastry bag. Delighted to find a cream cheese danish, I bit into the flaky crust as I contemplated the headline.

"What's up with you and Miss Elva? Seems like she's really embracing this whole reality show stuff. And just who is that nasty little man screaming at you on the cover?"

Relieved to move past any relationship talk, I narrowed my eyes down at Murray's little weasel face on the cover and shoved more of the danish into my mouth.

I rattled the bag to see if there were more pastries inside, and was rewarded with more options caught beneath the tissue paper at the bottom. "Miss Elva and I seem to be at odds because I might have mentioned that she was being selfish with all this publicity," I said.

Beau let out a gasp of surprise and leaned forward, taking the bag away from me before I ate all the pastries.

"You did not say that to her. I'm surprised she didn't annihilate you on the spot."

"I know, I know," I said, tossing the toy for Hank again and leaning back to pull my feet beneath me on the chair. "It's just that – she doesn't seem like herself. And we really need to pull together, not apart, with all these reporters sniffing around. Miss Elva claims it's good for business, but after the whole Pharma Boy drama, I'm ready for a quiet existence for a while."

"Maybe she's bored?" Beau asked, and I tilted my head at him in question. "You know, she's always busy helping others and doing her voodoo and whatnot, but maybe she just wanted something different for a bit."

"That's... actually, that's entirely a consideration. She hasn't dated anyone in ages, she's always available to help us with any problem we can't handle on our own, and she has seen and done it all. Maybe this was just something that was spicing up her life a bit," I considered, and then immediately felt shame wash over me for calling her self-ish. She'd saved my life on more than one occasion, which wasn't something a selfish person would do.

"I'm not saying her attitude doesn't need to be checked once in a while, but... just offering another take on things, I guess," Beau shrugged.

"Yeah, thanks. I'll see if maybe I can talk this through with her soon."

Beau checked his watch, a nice dive watch which I knew he wore not only for diving, but because it was waterproof and he wouldn't have to worry about it when he was tending bar or in the kitchen.

"I've got to get scooting, but tell me about this Dominick."

"Ugh. I'm more disgusted with his assistant, but since they're a package deal, I've decided to hate them both," I said, eying the pastry bag which Beau handed over with a smile. "Dominick is a psychic who wants to set up shop here and bring a 'real' psychic to Tequila Key. Murray's his little minion, who seems to think he also has great powers. Together, they want to storm the world and show everyone how great they are – both here in Tequila Key and on the reality show, I guess."

"And did you tell them to take their business and shove it you know where?" Amusement danced in Beau's eyes.

"I told them that as an entrepreneur, I think competition is healthy and invited them to set up shop."

"That's my girl. This stuff will settle out." Beau rose and bent to press a kiss to my cheek. "Don't let it overly fuss you. But you'd better make up with Miss Elva. She's the one who matters in all this."

"You're right. As always. Miss you so much," I said, standing and giving him a squeeze. "Thanks for giving me the heads up on this. At least I can prepare for the fall-out a bit more."

"You'll be just fine, Althea Rose. You're one of the ones who always lands on her feet."

Chapter Twelve

I MADE a mental note to stop by Miss Elva's on the way home as I rode my beach cruiser into work – early for once, thanks to Beau, and enjoying a highly caffeinated sugar buzz. Noting that the shutters were still closed on the little beach cottage we'd converted into the shop we have now, I patted myself on the back for arriving before Luna for once. Madonna's song "Like a Prayer" blared from my phone and I dug into my purse to see that my mother was calling me from whatever exotic locale she was currently stationed at.

"Is it the Maldives this time, or Tahiti? I can never keep it straight," I said by way of hello, and was rewarded with hearing her laugh.

"Actually, just a quick stop through Fiji. I've been commissioned by a few high-level clients that I can't discuss, but it's really delightful here. You should come join us." My mother, Abigail Rose, astrologer and psychic to the stars, was worried about me.

"That's quite a haul from here," I pointed out, winding

my bike chain through the wheel and locking it to the bike rack on the side of the cottage.

"It would do you wonders to have a vacation," Mom continued. "Such blue water and lovely diving here. And no photographers."

"You've seen the magazines," I sighed.

"Yes, well, you know, things get forwarded to me and your father. And we're both very concerned for you. But I've got a bad feeling about this Dominick Murray man. He's not reading well for me." My mother paused.

"Two men. Dominick, and his assistant Murray. Both of whom are impossibly full of themselves and seem to think they'll run me out of business."

"That's not going to happen," Mom said immediately, and I agreed with her insight.

"I doubt it as well. They're just pests right now. It'll be fine – I just kind of want things to settle down. I feel like I haven't had a chance to catch my breath in ages," I admitted, tugging the strap of my messenger bag up my shoulder. The sun was high enough now that I was beginning to break a sweat, so I needed to get moving inside.

"And you won't for a while. Watch yourself – especially around that Murray. I've got a bad feeling about him."

"Wait until you see the next magazine cover," I said, moving toward my side of the cottage, where I would go in through the side door.

"How bad? Oh, I don't like this. I really think you need to leave town, Althea." Mom was beginning to sound frazzled, which for her calm and collected self was downright frantic.

"I don't see that happening anytime soon. I promise, I'll get through this," I said, and with many kisses and promises to keep them updated, I ended the call and tried to shake the sense of dread that had washed over me. Granted, my mother's premonitions were usually dead on, but it was hard for me to shake the feeling that something was seriously wrong.

"Hey Herman," I said off-handedly to my skeleton, who was perched outside the door to my shop, his arms crossed over his chest and his head tilted at a cheeky angle. My hand was almost on the door when I froze.

"Shit."

Chapter Thirteen

I COULD SEE NOW what I probably would've noticed if I hadn't been distracted by promising my mother that I was fine and that, no, of course everything was just great. Because – judging by the fact that Herman was casually leaning against the wall *outside* the shop and my door was open a crack – things were most certainly not fine.

Now, here's the problem with me: I'm the curious sort. And I was just itching to push the door open to my shop and see what had happened. But at the same time, I was trying out this whole adulting thing, so the more common-sense approach would be to call the police and allow them to investigate so I didn't contaminate any evidence or whatever.

But it was my shop. I struggled for a second and pulled my phone back out to call Luna, pacing in front of the door as I waited for her to answer.

"What's wrong?" Luna asked immediately, having gotten a psychic flash of what was going on – or, at least, that was what I was assuming.

"I'm at the shop. Herman is outside and the door is partially open. I want to push it open but I'm also terrified of what I'll find inside." The words rushed out and my heart pounded in my chest.

"Call the police."

"But what if it isn't anything police-worthy? Like what if Trace left a surprise or something?"

"Does it feel that way?"

"No," I admitted, trying to see inside the door, but it was dark in my office. "I'm just going to nudge the door with my toe and see if anything's in there."

"Althea, just call the police and let them do it. In fact, I'm getting off the phone and doing it now. Don't do anything stupid," Luna warned, and disconnected.

So of course I did something stupid.

Nudging the door open with my foot, I danced back as it swung into the room, allowing the outside light to flood my office. Staying back, I hovered for a moment, waiting to see if anyone was going to come rushing out, guns blazing. When no such thing happened, I peeked inside.

Dominick sat in Herman's chair, his arms crossed over his chest, staring at me.

"What the hell? Listen, Dominick, this is taking things too far. You can't break into my –"

A flash of heat rushed through me – the kind you get right before the shock hits, almost like slamming an epipen into your heart before the adrenaline begins to shake your system.

Dominick wouldn't be answering any of my questions any time soon.

Or ever, really.

I should've listened to Luna.

Chapter Fourteen

"CAN you get that as your next tattoo, maybe?" Luna whispered in my ear. "'Listen to Luna.' You could have it done up in a nice script with some designs. That way in case you have to make a life decision – as in what would Luna do – you'd be reminded to make the Luna-approved choice."

"I didn't go inside, did I? I just looked," I pointed out from where we both sat in Luna's back room. Chief Thomas had confiscated our phones and told us to stay put. I was more than annoyed that he'd taken my phone, but I didn't really have a say in the matter. I supposed it was better than being hauled down to the station and shoved into an interrogation room.

"But then what kind of stories would you have for our office Christmas party?" I quipped and, despite myself, found myself choking back a giggle as Luna did the same. Soon we were convulsing in silent laughter, tears rolling down our faces, kind of like when you're in church or at a funeral and aren't supposed to make a sound, but find yourself breaking out in manic laughter.

Except, you know, we'd just found a dead body in our place of business.

Dominick had been perched in my chair, his body arranged so that it looked like he was staring at me, with no visible – at least to me – signs of injury. Instead of rushing in to check on him, I'd dropped my mental shields and tried to see if I could get any brain waves or energy coming from him. When I found nothing, I backed out of my shop without touching anything, and waited for Luna and the police. There was nothing I could have done to save him at that point.

"You ladies think this is funny?" Chief Thomas asked, sticking his head into the doorway, his handsome face lined in disapproval.

"No, we don't," I said, helplessly wiping my eyes. "But I think we're a little hysterical. The shock of it all is kind of setting in."

Chief Thomas's eyes were cool and assessing, but he nodded once without speaking. He motioned for us to stay where we were, then returned to the conversation he'd been having on his cell phone before he'd poked his head into the back room to check on us.

"I was going to question you ladies down at the station, but someone's broken the news already, and the media is like damn rats around cheese outside. We'll do the interviews here – but I'll need to record them. Is that all right?"

It was then that I really heard the pandemonium outside. Not only was Luna's backroom fairly soundproof due to the protection she needed for the magicks and spells she ran here, but I'd been purposely trying to avoid listening to anything outside the room.

A part of me didn't want to know how he'd died, or to think about his last moments – sitting in my leopard print chair, perhaps slowly realizing that the end was closing in. Or maybe he'd died elsewhere and was then deposited in my chair.

Damn it, I really loved that chair, and now I'd have to sell it. The lingering energy would be no good to have in my office. Speaking of which…

I turned to ask Luna what kind of protection magick she could run for me, but Chief Thomas had returned with his recorder. He closed the door behind him, drowning out some of the noise from outside.

"Reporters?"

"Like damn bloodthirsty mosquitos," Chief Thomas said, scowling down at his notepad as he flipped through the worn book until he found an empty page to take notes on. Setting up his iPhone between the both of us, he paused before turning it on, his eyes finally registering Luna's workroom. Meticulous as the rest of her shop, her backroom was packed with every magical ingredient, oddity, and everyday oils, salts, and natural ingredients she needed to create her potions, lotions, and elixirs. Every bottle and box was precisely labeled and dated, and though I knew Chief Thomas wouldn't understand, the moon symbol showed what type of moon each ingredient had been collected under. Luna's attention to detail and precision with her carefully-crafted products and magick was what made her items some of the top magickal retail products around the world.

I was just happy she'd pulled the rug over the pentagram etched on her floor.

"This is quite the space," Chief Thomas finally commented, and Luna dimpled up at him, carefully weaving her charming spell around the Chief.

"Thank you. I think it's vital to provide the best and most natural ingredients in all my products," Luna said, her charm like a blast of sunshine warming us all.

Chief nodded along. "I can see that. I have to say, your shop is real classy. Not something you'd expect from someone in your trade. I guess I was thinking it would be more like –" Chief Thomas realized he was about to insult me and stopped short.

"Like my shop?" I asked easily, crossing my legs in front of me. Both Luna and I sat on overstuffed cushions tossed on the floor beneath one of her tall narrow windows.

"I'm sorry. I certainly don't mean to offend," Chief Thomas said, a faint blush tinging his cheeks. I reminded myself that this man had put himself on the line for me more than once.

"It's okay. I tried making my side just as elegant as Luna's, but business tanked afterward. It seems people like the stereotypes that go along with psychics. I've learned it's better to meet and exceed expectations than it is to make people question themselves. Clients expect a shop full of oddities and psychic baubles, and I deliver. It may not make sense, but it helps business." I shrugged one shoulder.

"No, it makes sense. It would be like going to a greasy diner and being served caviar. I'd be mistrustful."

Not a metaphor I'd considered before, but it worked, so I just nodded my head.

"I am going to read you both your rights, you understand why, yes? It doesn't mean you're being accused of anything, but I will need to follow procedure here. This is strictly me being cautious – what with the press being all about the place."

Luna and I both nodded, but stayed silent while he read us our revised Miranda rights. I swear, it was awful being on the receiving end of that. I know the rights are there to protect you, but it still felt like we were being accused of a crime.

"I have to ask you both your whereabouts between two a.m. and four a.m. this morning," Chief Thomas asked. He had turned on his iPhone recorder and leaned against the wall, one booted foot crossed over the other, pen poised above his paper.

"I was sleeping at home," Luna said.

"Was anyone with you? I'm sorry if that's a delicate question, but I need to know if you were alone or not," Chief Thomas said.

"My boyfriend Mathias was with me. He'd arrived home around one o'clock or so from his ER shift, and then I think he was up going through emails, but I'm not sure how late," Luna said.

Chief Thomas noted it down, and then indicated that I should speak.

"I was at home, sleeping, and not very well," I admitted.

"Were you alone?" Chief Thomas asked.

"Yes, I was. Unless you count Hank, my dog," I said.

Chief Thomas smiled at that, but just shook his head. "Would anyone be able to verify what time you arrived home last night or when you left this morning?"

"Not really my arrival at home, unless one of my neighbors was on their porch. Beau stopped by my house this morning, so he'd be able to tell you that I was home."

"And what time was that?"

"Around sevenish, maybe?"

Chief Thomas made a note. "When did you last see the deceased?"

I swallowed against a throat that had gone dry. It was a question I had not been looking forward to.

"In the parking lot of Lucky's last night. We had a bit of an altercation," I said.

Chief Thomas did not register surprise, which just goes to show how quickly the small-town gossip chain worked.

"You and Dominick had an argument?" Chief Thomas clarified.

"Myself and his assistant, Murray. Dominick only appeared toward the end. Frankly, I had no problem with him, other than I thought he was pretentious and that he made poor hiring choices," I said.

"Why did you think he was pretentious? And what was the argument with Murray about?"

"I thought he was pretentious because he came into my shop a few days ago, unannounced, looked me and the shop over, declared that I was a hack and that he was going to take all my clientele, and left. As for his little minion – I mean, Murray, the man's obsessive and kind of a donkey. He acts like he thinks he's the next great psychic or something. We argued because he's trying to take a reality TV show that's been offered to Luna and me. Which neither of us wants to do, but I'm half-willing to do it just to keep him from being on it."

"Obsessive – how so?"

"Murray thinks his boss, as well as himself, are like the be-all, end-all of psychic readers." I shrugged and tugged on a teal curl. "As an entrepreneur, I think competition is healthy and good for business, and I told them so, and that I was fine with them opening a shop. Which is not the reaction they were expecting – I'm sure they were trying to ruffle my feathers some. But since then, Murray's been popping up wherever I go and I don't like it."

"He's stalking you?" Chief Thomas raised an eyebrow in question and made a note on his pad.

"I wouldn't say that quite yet. But he's keeping close tabs on us, yes."

"And there's a reality show that's coming down to Tequila Key? About psychics?" Chief Thomas looked positively pained at the thought of this, pinching the bridge of his nose for a moment.

"Correct," Luna said, stretching her legs in front of her as she adjusted herself on the cushion.

"You ladies have agreed to have cameras follow you around all day?" Chief Thomas asked.

Luna and I both shook our heads adamantly.

"No, sir. That's quite possibly the last thing either of us wants. After all the reporters who followed us during the Pharma Boy fiasco, I think we've had our fill of national news coverage," Luna said.

"I agree. I've no interest in being famous," I added.

Chief Thomas narrowed his eyes at me for a moment.

"Your mother's famous. Some might say that would make you feel the need to prove yourself, to her or others."

"Thank goodness I have a very calm and normal father," I said, smiling at the thought of my music professor father. "He's instilled a strong sense of normalcy in me, which was important considering the world in which I was raised. But here's the thing – I already know I could be famous if I wanted to be. My mother has invited me to join her repeatedly. I could read for all the stars and find out all their secrets, and travel the world doing so. I don't need a reality television show to get me there. It's just not the life I want. If, some day, I get bored – I'll go join her."

That seemed to satisfy Chief Thomas. He nodded along for a bit, made a few notes, and then, as the pandemonium outside grew, he glanced over his shoulder.

"Here's the deal, ladies. So far, everything checks out. It's unfortunate your boyfriend wasn't with you last night, Althea. I'm going to have to ask that you don't leave town anytime soon. However, I can't quite see you killing someone and leaving them in your place of employment to be found. Stay close for any questions, you hear me?"

"Of course. Whatever you need," I said, blowing out a breath. "Can you tell us how he died?"

"Inconclusive at the moment. No identifying marks or injury wounds that I could see. My guess will be some sort of toxin or poison. The coroner will be able to tell me more."

Chief Thomas looked around the room full of bottles and herbs, and back at Luna.

"Anything poisonous in here?"

"Not particularly," Luna said, "Nothing like a neuro-toxin or anything of the like. But I'm sure that some of the ingredients, if mixed in the wrong manner, could cause some damage."

"I appreciate the honesty. I need to go talk to the press. Stay close and available." He paused as he was about to leave the door, iPhone in hand. "Question – if you're a psychic, Althea, how come you didn't see this happening?"

I shrugged. It was a common misconception that psychics were able to predict every aspect of the future. In all reality, I got flashes of insight, or something like mini-movies that played out for me in my mind. For the most part, I kept myself mentally shielded so I could go about my day.

"I'm not sure I would really be living my life if I tried to foresee and predict every event that was coming my way. Some of what I do and who I am needs to be left to my reaction in the moment and how I feel. If I'm constantly anticipating a particular event that I foresaw in my head, then I'm not really reacting in the moment, am I? I'd just be projecting how I felt based on what I'd already seen, if that makes any sense. I've found that it's best to kind of put blinders up when it comes to my own life."

"You'd think after all the run-ins and threats you've had the last few months, you'd take those blinders down," Chief Thomas said as he left the room to deal with the increasingly loud din coming from outside.

The man had a point.

Chapter Fifteen

LUNA and I eased our way across her darkened shop, and I was grateful for the fact she'd still had her shutters closed. We peeked through the slit in one when we heard a scream.

"Murray," Luna breathed, and we huddled together behind the shutters and watched the drama unfold out front of our shop.

Dominick's mini-me, Murray, looked as disheveled as I'd seen him yet – and I'd seen him in many unflattering positions in our short acquaintance. With barely buttoned jeans and a tattered t-shirt he'd obviously slept in, his face had gone dead white behind the light tan he'd picked up over the last few days of being in the sun.

"What do you mean? I don't understand. This has to be some elaborate prank," Murray raged, pacing back and forth next to a harried-looking police officer who kept smoothing his hair nervously as his eyes darted at the hovering cameras. The police officer put his hand on

Murray's shoulder and murmured something that caused rage to cross Murray's face. He threw the officer's hand off and stalked in front of our shop, tears glistening in his eyes.

"I demand to know what happened. I need answers now." Spittle flew from his lips as he cursed, clearly not concerned that the reporters would have to edit it out, and Chief Thomas stepped forward to address him.

"I'm sorry for your loss," Chief Thomas began, and Murray whirled on him.

"Sorry? Sorry doesn't even begin to cut it. I want these women locked up for what they've done. He… he was my best friend." Murray's voice cracked and he swiped a tear angrily from his eye with the back of his fist.

"I understand the two of you worked together as well?" Chief Thomas consulted his notebook. "You were his assistant?"

Murray drew himself up in disgust. "I was more than his assistant – I was his protégé. We both understood that the real power lay with me. He was only grooming and mentoring me to launch my career into the stratosphere."

Glancing at Luna, I caught her eye roll and mirrored it back. The little twit didn't have even half the power and presence Dominick had wielded. Chief Thomas didn't seem to know how to respond to that, so he just made a note in his notebook and cleared his throat.

"I can't release any details at this time, until the medical examiner gives me more information. Also, next of kin needs to be notified. I'd appreciate it if you all –" he looked around at the reporters – "would give us at least an hour so we can call his family."

"I am his family," Murray declared, and Chief Thomas nodded again.

"I understand you feel that way, but unless you are his power of attorney, his next of kin will need to make some choices."

Murray didn't seem to know what to say to that, and he seemed to deflate from within, his hands clenching in anger as he scanned our shop again. It was when his eyes landed on the slit in the blind that he really went ballistic.

"It was those two! They did this!"

Luna and I jumped back from the window, letting the slit fall closed, but all eyes and cameras had turned to us. In seconds, a hysterical Murray was banging at our door, his shouts echoing across the porch.

"Murderers!" Murray shrieked.

"I think this would be a good time to go out the back door," Luna murmured, and I agreed with her. Chief Thomas hadn't asked us to stay – he'd simply requested that we don't leave town. I'd just make sure the CSI team – and by 'team' I meant two people – would lock up after. Poking my head in the room, I asked if they could do so, and they barely nodded from where they were doing their thing. I couldn't help but wonder how many fingerprints or stray hairs they would collect from town. It could be a veritable who's who of murder suspects if they really started going deep into any DNA analysis.

We eased quietly out the back door, hoping the majority of the press would stay where the real show was – with Murray and his hysterics on the front porch. We'd almost made it to Luna's Mini when a distraught shriek reached us and Murray rounded the corner, having been tipped off by a member of the press who had stepped across the street to take a wide-angle shot of our business.

"Oh shit," Luna said.

Oh shit, indeed.

Chapter Sixteen

CHIEF THOMAS CAUGHT Murray two steps before he got his hands around my neck, in a flying tackle worthy of a stadium full of cheers. I gaped down at the two as they skidded across the gravel of the parking lot, wincing as Murray's head cracked the rocks.

"Do not move," Chief Thomas threatened Murray, who, despite his smaller size, bucked against Chief Thomas's considerable strength. It was only when Murray's shoulders began to shake that Chief Thomas decided to ease up the pressure and let Murray go.

"Dominick's dead," Murray wheezed, kneeling in the gravel. For a moment, looking at his torn shirt and the trickle of blood that wound its way down his forehead through his tears, I felt bad for him. Until he looked me dead in the eye and raised a finger at my face.

"I know you murdered him," Murray hissed, turning the finger back to tap his head. "I can see it in my head. I'm very powerful, you know."

Flashbulbs lit around us and I could all but feel the cameras recording every second of this nonsense.

"You're obviously not that powerful, as it's laughable to think I would kill anyone. I have nothing but respect for the sanctity of human life," I shot back, fed up with this little shit. A part of me wished he'd been the one murdered. I immediately mentally apologized to the goddess for having such thoughts. That was one of the things I'd always respected about myself and my family and friends – no matter what type of craft or spiritual powers we wielded, we never wished death upon anyone, no matter how much we disliked them. First, because a wish could often take on a life of its own, especially for those who are used to carrying magickal powers; and second, it's just bad karma. The universe has a way of sorting things out without any additional negative thoughts being stirred into the pot.

"I know things. Deep and powerful things. I see the future and I see the past," Murray seethed, jabbing his finger at his face. "And I know you killed Dominick."

"You can say you 'know' all you want – but what you're doing right now is maligning my friend's reputa-tion, and if you don't back off I'm happy to sue you for slander," Luna said, her voice steely though she looked every inch a perturbed pixie. I knew she'd look as light as air on television next to me, and the whole world would eat her up. Cate wasn't wrong to assume we'd be good on a television show. We were the perfect foils for each other.

"I don't care. Justice is what matters. Justice for my brother and my best friend." Murray raised his hands to the sky and the reporters almost laughed, but they all knew good television when they saw it. Chief Thomas just pinched the bridge of his nose and I felt sorry for him. I could see how being a police officer was at times a thankless job.

"Maybe you should stop talking, then, and let the chief do his job so justice can be served?" I asked, examining my nails as if I didn't have a care in the world.

"Shut up, you murderer," Murray said.

I shook my head sadly at him. "You're the one stopping the chief from doing his job. Don't you think his time would be better served collecting information? Like, for instance, where you were last night?" I asked, fed up with Murray's nonsense and wanting to get out of the sun, which was beginning to send trickles of sweat down my back.

"I'll be the one doing the interrogating, Ms. Rose," Chief Thomas said, addressing me formally. That was probably very smart of him, though it kind of annoyed me to be called out in front of the reporters.

"Oh, this one can accuse me of murder but I can't ask where he was last night?" I scoffed, and one of the reporters nodded in agreement with me. They were enjoying every second of this and the less they had to fight for information, the easier their job was.

"Everyone, just stop. I don't have the time or inclination to stand out here and squabble with everyone. Murray, you're coming with me. I have some questions for you. Ms. Rose and Ms. Lavelle, I'll be in touch. The shop stays closed until I say so."

"You're just going to let them walk?" Murray's voice rose until he sounded like a tea kettle steaming.

"I can't hold them because you say you've had a psychic vision. The judge would get real fussy with me if I started submitting that as evidence in lieu of, you know, facts and evidence," Chief Thomas said dryly. "I also find it highly unlikely that these two women would murder someone and leave the body in their shop for us to find."

Okay, so Chief Thomas was back in my good graces for standing up for us. Murray struggled to his feet, gasping with the effort, and his entire body shook as he raised his finger at us once more – which I was now absolutely certain was for the cameras.

"But don't you see? It's the perfect crime. They left his body in their place of business for exactly that reason – to look like they'd been framed. Now they can play the shocked and saddened victims, while in all reality they're cold-blooded killers."

The picture that ran that night showed my face in black and white – a mask of disgust – as I lunged toward a sobbing Murray whose finger pointed at me in accusation.

Who was I kidding? I'd buy a magazine with that cover in a hot minute.

Chapter Seventeen

"JUST BREATHE, THEA," Luna soothed, patting me on the shoulder where I sat, head between my legs, trying not to hyperventilate at the latest magazine cover. We were hanging at my house that evening, much to Hank's delight, and I was several shots of tequila deep already. Don't judge – it's what one does when one's picture is splashed across newspapers with the word *murderer* followed by a question mark.

"Seriously, I don't understand how magazines are printing things so fast. Is this like a special edition? This happened this morning. I can't keep up with this digital age. They must have, like, robots from alien worlds building these things." I hiccupped and realized I was dangerously close to tears.

Hank stuck his head between my knees and slurped his tongue across my face in one long, solid lick – startling me enough to swallow a hiccup and pull my head up. "Ewww, Hank." I found myself smiling down at my bouncy dog. This is why they called the dog 'man's best friend,' I thought, and scratched behind Hank's ears. A knock at the door sent him scrambling and Luna leapt to follow him across my room. Reporters had been camped out on my stoop once again, and the last thing I needed was having my picture taken when I was half in the bag on tequila.

I was pretty certain my neighbors were ready to have me kicked out of the neighborhood. They'd seen more action on this dead-end street – from reporters and riff-raff coming through to bother me – in the last six months than they had in years. If I didn't own the place, I was certain they'd be petitioning my landlord to evict me.

Squinting, I shut one eye and carefully poured myself another shot of tequila, but let it sit. I hadn't eaten since morning, and I was close to hitting my limit with the alcohol. Instead, I stretched and tried to remember what I had for food in my freezer, but desperately hoped that Trace had thought to bring food instead. He'd called after getting off a long day of diving, and would be on his way over once he'd finished cleanup.

"Takeout delivery," Luna called, her voice decidedly sing-song, and I narrowed my eyes in suspicion. When Miss Elva came out on the patio, her arms full of bags of food from Lucky's, I couldn't decide if I was still annoyed with Miss Elva, happy to see her, happy to see the food, or annoyed that I'd have to talk through a relationship issue with a friend when all I wanted to do was eat some greasy food and let my mind chill for a bit after the whirlwind day I'd had.

"Now, don't be shooting me that pussface, child. You always get cranky when you don't eat. I've brought you all your favorites, courtesy of Beau, and you'll eat them before you drink one more ounce of tequila. Then you and I will be having ourselves a little chat."

I considered all angles of that, reminded myself that I was adulting this week, and nodded my assent. Wisely keeping my mouth shut, I tore into a bag of crispy fried pickles and almost moaned in delight. Beau added a hint of Cajun spice to the batter and they were to die for. The three of us ate in companionable silence, all seeming to agree that there was a time for airing our grievances and a time for honoring the holiness that is greasy comfort food. The only sound that interrupted our worship was Hank's joyful barking as he chased an increasingly annoyed Rafe around the house.

For reasons we had yet to ascertain, Hank had no trouble seeing Rafe. And, much to Rafe's dismay, Hank was convinced that Rafe was sent to play with him. I liked to think he considered Rafe some zippy chew toy that flitted through the air for the sole purpose of entertainment.

"Devil beast! Enough!" Rafe's voice reached a whiny, high-pitched note, which was typically when I intervened.

"Hank," I called, wielding the holy grail of comfort food. "French fry!"

Hank skidded around the corner, all but falling over himself in his excitement. It was like all his Christmases had come at once – a Rafe chew toy and a French fry. If a dog could reach nirvana, Hank was pretty darn close.

Rafe floated behind him, straightening his hat and running a hand over his disheveled mustache.

"Devil beast," Rafe said again, to nobody in particular, and I just shrugged my shoulder.

"Nobody said you had to come over. You knew Hank would be here," I said.

"I go where Miss Elva goes," Rafe said, his face set in stubborn lines.

"Have you tried being friends with him? Maybe you guys could end up being buddies if you put a little effort in," Luna suggested, and I secretly hoped that would never happen. With as much lip as Rafe gave us on a daily basis, it gave me no end of joy to see him terrorized by the twenty-five pounds of fluff that lived under my roof.

"Friends? With a dog? Doubtful," Rafe sniffed, but he glanced down at Hank with new consideration in his eyes.

"Speaking of friends…" Luna said, and gestured between Miss Elva and me – which immediately made me wonder if she'd been the one to set up this little meeting. Giving her the stink eye, I delicately sipped at my tequila instead of downing the shot in one.

"Don't you look at her like that," Miss Elva said, straightening her caftan, which was deep purple with delicate red poppies etched up the side. "This was my idea. Once I saw all the hullabaloo with that dead psychic and your face on the screen, I knew Miss Elva was needed. Even if you've been bitchy lately, a friend is a friend, I say. So here I am, bearing comfort food and letting you know I'm here to help."

As apologies went, it was a fairly convoluted one – and not actually, once I worked my way past the 'bitchy' comment, an apology. Struggling for composure, I took a few deep breaths and practiced my adult voice.

"Do you understand why I've been unhappy with your

behavior lately?" There; that was as non-accusatory as I could summon at the moment.

Miss Elva blew out a breath and leaned back on the cushions, patting the spot next to her so Hank could jump up and she could run her hand down his back. Her soulful brown eyes looked out across the yard, where the sun was beginning to set low on the horizon.

"Child, I understand. I was getting myself a little caught up in the whole fame thing. I know I wasn't being true to myself or who I am. It's just that…" Miss Elva's face grew wistful for a moment.

I paused, a French fry halfway to my mouth, as I was certain for half a second that Miss Elva was going to shed a tear.

"Are you…"

"No, child, I am not going to cry," Miss Elva said, reaching for my shot and downing it in one gulp. "You didn't see me about to cry, did you?"

Luna shook her head. "No ma'am. I think the pollen count is up this week. I've had the worst allergies."

"That's right. It has been thick this week, hasn't it? Now, what I was saying before Miss Thang here rudely interrupted me –" Miss Elva glared at me and I held my hands up in the go-ahead gesture – "is that sometimes I get bored… or restless, I guess. I've lived a hell of a life, but much of it the past years has been in this sleepy little town. And my gifts and talents are often under-appreciated here. I suppose when I saw a chance to shake things up a bit, add some spice, I just kind of ran with it. It was fun for a bit, but I realize now that fame isn't what I really wanted. I'd be just as happy with taking a nice vacation or meeting up with your mother, Althea, on one of her jaunts around the globe. Just to kick my heels up a bit," Miss Elva said.

And just like that, any lingering annoyances or resentment I'd had with Miss Elva were gone.

"I understand," I said, pouring her another tequila, but she shook her head and declined. I knew she preferred beer and would go rummage in my fridge soon enough. "For a moment there, when Cate was offering us the reality show, I thought about taking it. Maybe it would be fun, or introduce me to new people – or hey, maybe we'd make a ton of dough off of it. I can see the appeal. But ultimately, I like my life. And I think fame limits you and the lifestyle you live much more than we realize. I'd be miserable if cameras followed me around all day long. I can barely get myself put together and out the door to work every morning. If I had to consider that my picture would be taken every time I left the house? Yeah, I'd turn into one of those phone psychics who charge by the minute and never leave."

Miss Elva snorted. "Which you'd be shit at."

"Total shit," I agreed.

We laughed, the tension around us floating away, and soon enough we were back in our groove. Miss Elva had an ice-cold Corona, I still had my tequila, and Luna had switched to a glass of crisp white wine. The sun had just set, and for a moment I was able to pretend like we were just three girlfriends hanging out on the porch on a warm, muggy evening.

"He doesn't want to be my friend," Rafe wailed as he raced around the corner, an exuberant Hank bounding across the yard after him.

Well, us girls and our pirate ghost, I thought with a smile. It just about made me forget about the reporters camped out front.

"Can you run in circles please? It will tire him out," I called to Rafe, who shouted an obscenity back at me that no Southern lady would dare to repeat.

"Tell me about today," Miss Elva said, and I filled her in on all that had transpired. I will say this about Miss Elva – she's an excellent listener. But for a few "mm"s, she didn't interrupt once until we'd finished filling her in.

"That assistant of his is guilty," Miss Elva said immediately.

Both Luna and I drew back in surprise. "How do you know? What do you see?"

"I don't know quite yet. I'd have to be in person to really get a read on him. He's guilty of something. Not the murder, maybe, but he's guilty of… something that caused it? Led to it? I don't know. He has a part, but I can't see what or how. I know that I don't like him, though," Miss Elva said.

"That's a given. He's a power-hungry little narcissist. Like one of those tiny short guys that drives a screamingly-yellow Hummer or Porsche to prove his manhood," I grumbled.

"What can we do to gather more information? Should we find Murray and see if you can get a read on him? Or you, Althea, when he isn't busy shouting at you? I know it's hard for you to get a clear picture when he's getting you all worked up," Luna said, sipping her wine and tucking her bare feet under her on the chair.

"Virtually impossible. I'm not an open vessel allowing

psychic imagery to flow through me. I'm more like a spit-ting mad cat that just got dunked in bathwater," I admitted.

"First, let's get near Murray so I can get a read. But the easiest way would be to do a soul level reenactment," Miss Elva mused, tapping one finger against her lips as she thought.

"Like act out the murder?" Confusion filled me; we didn't even know how the man was murdered. How were we supposed to reenact his death?

Miss Elva's big booming chuckle rolled over us and I grinned at her, happy we were at peace again. Even better than comfort food was Miss Elva, my very own personal comfort blanket.

"No, as in with magick. It's an ancient and very specific ritual. The trickiest part is that you need to get permission from the deceased's spirit first. For many reasons, they may not want to reveal their last moments to someone."

"Like what?" I wondered.

"If it could implicate a loved one, if they are still in shock about being murdered, if they or a loved one would come to harm – things like that," Miss Elva explained.

I nodded in understanding. "Okay, step one. Get permission from Dominick's ghost. Got it," I said, squinting at the tequila bottle again. This definitely sounded like something I would need more tequila to wrap my head around. Picking up my shot glass, I took another small sip.

"Yes, which is only the first ritual. After you've received clear permission from their spirit, then you'll need to do the next sacred ritual, in which the deceased's spirit will actually walk through and relive their last moments for you. It's kind of like watching a movie play out before you," Miss Elva explained. "You aren't in the scene or anything, but you might as well be. It's all very real and graphic."

"Lovely," I murmured, downing the tequila and wondering if I would ever sleep again after having to watch someone get murdered in real-time live-action in front of me.

"It's not for the faint of heart, that's for sure. But if you're going to be implicated in a murder, I suggest we get to it as quickly as possible. It's a full moon tomorrow night, which will be perfect timing as the veil is extra thin. I'll gather the ingredients, and the spells are in my books at home," Miss Elva said.

We all turned at another knock at the door, Hank beel-ining in joy across the room.

"Trace is coming over," I explained, getting up and moving on unsteady legs across the room. Peeking out the door, I was less than delighted to see Chief Thomas at the door.

"Come in," I said, hiding behind the door and closing it quickly after he entered. Chief Thomas scooted in quickly and then took his hat off in his hands, looking decidedly unhappy.

"What's happened?" I breathed.

He looked past me and cleared his throat.

"Medical examiner's results came in. Is Miss Elva here?"

"Yes, but what does that have to do with anything? What did the results show?" I turned as Luna and Miss

Elva entered the room. They both stopped when they saw my stricken look and Chief Thomas twisting his hat in his hands. Rafe hovered behind them, mirroring Chief Thomas's actions with his own hat.

"Miss Elva, I'm going to have to read you your rights. You're under arrest for the murder of Dominick St. Germain…"

Chapter Eighteen

PANDEMONIUM HIT the minute Chief Thomas walked Miss Elva to the waiting squad car. The front of my house looked like a rave, with flashes going off a mile a minute and reporters shouting questions at Chief Thomas, who waved everything away with a simple, "No comment."

I blamed Cate for all of this.

Not that there was any rationale behind that thought, except that if something like this had happened without national coverage from gossip magazine reporters who'd been shipped down here to follow a reality show in the making, there would have been only a reporter or two covering this for the local newspaper. Sad as it is to say, dead bodies just didn't rate the same coverage they once did in local news. Our nation was becoming desensitized to violence. However, if there was a juicy headline that involved warring psychics, magic spells, and the chance to call any one of us crazy or insane – especially the women – well, that would make a more enticing headline.

"Don't you hate it when people call women crazy?" I asked Luna. We'd muscled our way through the crowd as best we could and were currently cruising slowly behind Chief Thomas's squad car to the station. I wasn't ready to think about or address just why they had taken Miss Elva in. Chief Thomas had refused to comment, and I knew he'd just wanted to get away from my house and the reporters quickly. Luckily, he'd been willing to allow us to follow him to the station. After instructions to call her attorney and a quick side note on where she'd hidden her spell books, Miss Elva had said nothing else. A distraught Rafe ranted in the backseat of Luna's car, but he kept it largely to a whisper.

"What do you mean? Some women are crazy," Luna pointed out.

I looked out the window at the passing houses, tiny cottages, and single-story homes, their patio lights offering a warm glow in the darkness.

"Well, so are some men. But what I mean is that in general, the media and the all-encompassing 'they' use the term 'crazy' anytime a woman has emotions, or speaks up for herself, or is rightfully angry about something. Like, for example, when a woman loses it when her man cheats – then the guy is just all, 'well, you know, bitches be crazy' or whatever, and it totally dismisses the fact that she has a right to be angry. It's a way of minimizing women. I don't think women should be considered crazy for allowing ourselves to feel and process our emotions instead of forcing ourselves to logic our way through them."

Luna looked at me like I was the crazy one for a

moment, and perhaps I was. Maybe it was the tequila talking, but it was keeping me from going into panic mode over Miss Elva getting arrested.

"You're right, actually, though your timing for this conversation is a bit odd. I agree that the term 'crazy' is used to keep women down," Luna said. "And, frankly, if more men in our society were taught to process their emotions and not just shove them down, we'd have fewer mass shootings. It seems like every day there's another shooting by some man who's fed up with something and has never been taught to deal with frustration or anger in his life. And yet women are the crazy ones for articulating their emotions? What's so wrong with expressing that you're angry about something? I'd rather people do it with their words than with guns. Now that's crazy to me."

I realized she was just as anxious as I was about Miss Elva, as we were having a fairly deep conversation in an effort to avoid discussing what we were about to walk into.

My phone beeped with a text from Trace, asking where I was. The next text was from Miss Elva's attorney, who was on her way to the station. It still surprised me to find out Miss Elva had things like an attorney or an investment portfolio. It was easy sometimes to underestimate Miss Elva or take her at face value, but that woman had more layers than an onion.

"Women are crazy. I can tell you both that none of you have changed for centuries. You all were crazy years ago and you're still crazy," Rafe chimed in from the back seat. I'd almost forgotten he was still with us.

"Weird, men have changed so much," I said.

Rafe nodded enthusiastically. "They have. See, we're adaptable creatures. We evolve," he said, "while women continue to cook and clean for their men and throw tantrums when the men spend time with more than one woman. Nothing's really changed.

I glanced at Luna, begging her with my eyes to run the spell that would banish Rafe forever.

"No, Althea. Miss Elva would be mad," she said, and I sighed.

"You're lucky, pirate. I was about to show you just how much more power women have in this day and age," I grumbled, then turned my attention back to Chief Thomas, who waved us to a spot in the gated parking lot and then closed it behind us so the reporters wouldn't descend on the station like ants.

"I wouldn't normally allow you two in the station, but I have more questions for the both of you as well. We've got a tricky situation on our hands," Chief Thomas said as he opened the door and motioned for Miss Elva to get out of the back seat. He'd been kind enough to not put cuffs on her, which I knew was a serious breach of procedure. But I think even he knew that Miss Elva was not a flight risk.

Plus, the man had to live in this town. He knew it was best not to get on Miss Elva's bad side. Something had pushed him to make this arrest, though, and I wondered just what it was. I opened my mouth to ask, but Chief Thomas just lifted his chin toward where car doors were slamming on the street.

"Everyone inside. Interrogation Room A. We'll talk there."

Like Tequila Key had more than one interrogation

room, I thought, but wisely kept my mouth shut as we slipped in the side door of the station.

Maybe I was learning how to do this whole mature adult thing. If all it meant was that I had to keep my mouth shut, I figured I could do that once in a while.

Chapter Nineteen

MISS ELVA'S attorney was in the front office by the time we got settled into the interrogation room, and I stood and offered her my seat when she entered the room.

A no-nonsense woman with pretty brown skin, hair slicked back into a tight bun, and wearing a beautifully cut navy linen suit with a crisp white blouse, Verity Morgan took control the moment she entered the room.

"Verity Morgan," she said, introducing herself to Chief Thomas. He shook her hand and then we all introduced ourselves. Intelligence snapped in her eyes, and a level of take-no-bullshit that made me promise myself to call this woman should I ever land myself in any kind of trouble. I briefly wondered if I could hire her to whip my life into shape.

"Chief Thomas, please explain the allegations and why you've taken the step of arresting my client without so much as an interrogation," Verity began, crossing toned legs and pulling out a leather portfolio and a gold pen for taking notes.

"Interview on," Chief Thomas said, hitting his recorder and leaning back to pinch the bridge of his nose. "As you know, we are investigating a murder scene here. At the moment, Miss Elva is our top suspect. The medical examiner's report has been returned to me, and while we don't have the full autopsy reports yet, there were some interesting things to note. I'd like to ask some questions about that – of all of you ladies sitting here." Chief Thomas listed off our names for the recording and announced that we had all been read our rights before continuing, "First of all, do these markings mean anything to you?"

Chief Thomas slid a piece of paper across the desk and we all bent over to stare at a series of lines and dots drawn in a pattern.

"It's a ritual marking. Typically used to help spirits cross into the other realm," Miss Elva said evenly, not batting an eye when Chief Thomas's eyebrows raised in surprise.

"This would be voodoo? Something you practice?"

"It's not specific to voodoo. More of a pagan-white witch-voodoo mix of things. Ultimately, as you practice more and learn your strengths and weaknesses, you can weave many different elements into your rituals," Miss Elva explained. "Kind of like if you were a chef and took baking classes or learned how to roll sushi. One isn't better than the other, and all elements can be incorporated to achieve the final result that you're looking for."

"Would this ritual kill him?" Chief Thomas wore a look of incredulity at the fact that he was actually asking such a question.

Miss Elva looked at the chief like he'd lost his mind.

"No. None of our magick is used or meant for harm. 'Harm none' is the code by which we live our lives. Any black magick or dark magick will be returned to you three-fold. These here markings –" Miss Elva pointed at the paper – "they are put on the body after the person has died but the soul hasn't left yet. It's meant as a closure, a peaceful prayer, or a way to ease what can sometimes be a harsh transition for the soul. Those aren't my marks though – and from the looks of it – are quite fake."

Chief Thomas let that sit for a moment, and Verity jumped in.

"You're telling me that you're accusing my client of murder – an extremely serious allegation – based on some voodoo marks on the deceased's body?"

"That's not the only reason, no, but I wanted some clarification on what I was dealing with," Chief Thomas said. "Next question – do you know what the drug aconite is?"

I shook my head no, but both Luna and Miss Elva nodded.

"Luna, I've seen your storehouse of jars containing all manner of herbs and liquids. Do you carry this drug?"

"No, I don't. It has no use in the elixirs I make for people," Luna said.

"Miss Elva, if we searched your house, would we find this drug?" Chief Thomas asked.

Miss Elva shook her head in dissent. "Child, please, that's nasty stuff and of no use to me," she sniffed, offended that the chief had even asked.

"And yet you both know what the drug is," he pointed out.

"Knowledge of how a gun works doesn't mean someone used a gun," Verity said, and Chief Thomas nodded in agreement.

"I understand that. It's just kind of a very specific drug and something I don't see a lot of people having any knowledge about. And yet, here in this room are two practitioners of magicks who both have knowledge of this poison."

"We both take our craft and our business very seriously," Luna said, her tone dead serious as she met Chief Thomas's eyes dead on. "It would be highly irresponsible of either of us to not educate ourselves on which ingredients and elements to use in our magicks – and even more specifically what not to use. I'd even go so far as to say knowing what is harmful is more important than what is helpful. Shouldn't a doctor know which medicine will stop a man's heart in an instant versus what will ease the pain of a headache?"

We all tilted our heads and pursed our lips in question at Chief Thomas, and he held his hands up.

"Fair point. I suppose it's not something I know much about."

"Chief Thomas, are you saying that the deceased was poisoned, then? Is that the official cause of death?" Verity asked, making a note in her portfolio.

"Yes, official cause of death is aconite poisoning, though we have more testing to do. No other marks on his body indicating struggle or violence," he said.

"You do understand that you'll need to release my client, correct? Unless you have more evidence. Everything you've presented here today is circumstantial at best," Verity said, her gaze boring into Chief Thomas's.

A look of weariness, I might even say sadness flitted briefly across the chief's face before he turned to Miss Elva.

"Miss Elva, can you tell me where you were at roughly two fifteen this morning?"

"You don't have to answer that," Verity said immediately. "Or, if you'd like, we can have a chat before you answer any further questions."

The room went quiet and Miss Elva met Chief Thomas's eyes.

"I was leaving Dominick's hotel room. Where he'd been alive, living and breathing, and – by my assessment – a very happy man."

Chapter Twenty

I FINALLY UNDERSTOOD the phrase 'you could hear a pin drop.' Not that I'd had trouble understanding it before, but it was like all the air had been sucked out of the room as we all froze, aside from Miss Elva, who looked unflappable as usual.

"I really must insist that we pause the interview so I can have a conversation with my client so she understands the gravity of what she's saying," Verity began, but Miss Elva waved her away.

"I haven't done anything wrong and I don't have anything to hide. But I want you here to make sure Chief Thomas does everything by the book," Miss Elva said. "So when it comes out that I'm innocent, they can't say it was because everything wasn't on the up and up."

Verity looked pained, but finally squared her shoulders and gave Chief Thomas a look that would freeze ice. "How did you know my client was in the deceased's hotel room? There must be some sort of concrete evidence for you to have taken the step to arrest her," she said, pinning him with a look that said she would take no bullshit.

"We had an anonymous email with a video file attached," Chief Thomas said, turning his laptop around to pull up the video. A black and white security image showed a freeze frame of the Palms Inn, a cheerful little motel on the edge of town. Chief Thomas hit play and we all watched as one of the doors, marked with a large parrot, opened and Miss Elva stepped out. She was positively radiating good cheer as she swung herself down the hallway with an extra swing in her hips.

I bit my lip as Rafe went ballistic behind me, and did my best not to look over my shoulder. Luna straightened but kept her expression impassive as we both watched the video on repeat.

"My love mountain! How could she leave me to be with... that poor excuse for a man? I can't... such betrayal! And here I've been nothing but loyal to you. My love mountain. How could you. Do. This. To. Me."

It took everything in my power not to roll my eyes as Rafe flitted from the room, a ball of rage and ruffled feathers.

Were we not being interviewed or you know, sitting with someone who was assessing our sanity, I would have loved to address a few points in Rafe's rant, the first of which was that Miss Elva had told Rafe on more than one occasion that she would indulge in the pleasures of the flesh as it suited her and that she was not a one-man woman. Rafe had seemed to take it in stride at the time, even praising Miss Elva for thinking like a pirate and agreeing that one should always have more than one tasty treat to sample. It seemed he was singing a different tune now that he was on the receiving end of the situation.

Who was the crazy one now?

"That looks like a woman who has just had herself some fun with a man," Verity pointed out, and I watched the video along with everyone else once more.

"Or has just killed off someone who was presenting a challenge in her life," Chief Thomas said.

And, if I was being honest, it could really go either way. I thought about how much joy someone could take in offing a little rat like Murray – would they be whistling and humming as they strolled away from disposing of that particular annoyance in their life? On the flip side, as Rafe had stated earlier, a well-sexed woman is usually a happy one.

I was still tripping over the fact that Miss Elva had been in Dominick's room last night and hadn't breathed a word of it to us. The woman sure did play her cards close to her chest, I thought, trying to decide if I was upset with her or not. In the end, I decided I wasn't upset; my suspicion was that Miss Elva didn't tell us for exactly the reason we were all sitting in this interrogation room at the moment. The more knowledge we had, the more trouble we could get in.

But… still. Her and Dominick? How had that even come about?

It looked like we were about to find out.

Chapter Twenty-One

"DOMINICK and I have a bit of a... history," Miss Elva began, and I felt my eyebrows raise up to about my hairline.

"You look surprised by this, Althea," Chief Thomas noted for the record.

"I... uh, well, yeah. But I certainly understand if Miss Elva doesn't want to share all her past lovers with us," I said.

"Who has that kind of time?" Miss Elva wondered, and everyone in the room bit their lips to keep from laughing, Chief Thomas included.

"Um, you're saying that you and Dominick were intimate in the past as well as last night?" Chief Thomas said, doing his best to bring the interrogation back on track.

"Correct. I met him years ago on a trip to Miami for one of the big crystal and psychic conventions they do. You know, where people have booths and you can learn about services or pick up some new crystals, that kind of thing." Miss Elva waved her hand.

"Like a trade show?"

"Exactly." Miss Elva nodded. "And Dominick was there – without that nasty little assistant of his. I'm not sure when he acquired that one, but as I told him last night, he'd do well to be rid of him."

"You didn't like the assistant –" Chief Thomas consulted his notes – "Murray?"

"Nah, he is a loser. You can always tell the winners in life. Dominick was going places. He had some real talent. Both in and out of the bedroom." Miss Elva grinned and a trace of sadness flitted across her face. "It's a damn shame he's lost to us now, but he'll carry on his soulful duties in the next realm."

Chief Thomas looked like he was going to delve into that for a moment but, seeming to realize just how far off track that might take him, he let it pass.

"And how long did you know him for?"

"Child, like how long I know most of my men for – one night is about all I'll allow." Miss Elva chuckled her deep chuckle and I fought to keep a smile off my face. "We had some wine, some delicious Italian food, and a delightful romp in a pretty hotel room with a view over the water. We parted as friends and I've heard nothing from him until he came to town this week. When he realized I lived here, he stopped by to say hello, but it was a madhouse with all the reporters at my house. We agreed to meet up later and, well, one thing led to another. You know, for old times' sake," Miss Elva said.

"For the record then – you had nothing to do with the marks on his body?"

"Child, the only marks on his body might be some

bruising or bite marks from loving with a no-holds-barred woman such as myself. But I like my sex like I like my coffee – strong, straight up, and with no unnecessary additives. Magick doesn't play a role in my sex life, nor do rituals of any kind. It would be an offense to my powers to use them in that way." Miss Elva paused, and then pursed her lips as she thought about it. "Unless, I suppose, I was a sex witch. But I'm not."

Chief Thomas's face flushed and he opened his mouth to question her, but caught me and Luna vigorously shaking our heads no.

"I'll, uh, let that pass. Tell me about the last time you saw the deceased," he ordered.

I was still reeling from the fact that we were so calmly discussing Miss Elva's sex life, but I suppose stranger things have happened to me in the last few months.

"I saw him naked, sprawled on his bed, lighting up a cigarette even though you aren't supposed to smoke in those cute little rooms. Which I told him as much, since the proprietor, Jean, doesn't much like it when people break her rules. He laughed at me and promised to open a window. I told him not to get up, patted his cheek, and he said something about seeing me this week or seeing me soon. I told him if he was lucky." Miss Elva stilled at that. "Which is quite rude, now that I know he's dead. But it's what I said, so that's that. I expected I would see him around town, as he did tell me he'd taken a liking to the area and was interested in scouting out locations for his shop. To be honest, I didn't think he'd really do it. I saw him trying to get on this reality show and then moving on to somewhere bigger – fancier. He was a restless one." Miss Elva shrugged.

"The last you saw, he had no voodoo marks and was indeed alive?" Chief Thomas clarified.

"Correct. The man was alive and cheerful as could be – maybe a little bit sleepy."

Chief Thomas looked torn on how to proceed next.

"It's obvious someone else came into his room, then, no?" I asked. "Or that he left? Because somewhere in the next few hours he got from the Palms Inn to my office, and ended up dead."

"I hate to say this, Miss Elva, but I think I'm going to need to keep you in custody until your story checks out. You can certainly petition the judge to post bail, but it's a weekend and you know how those things go." Chief Thomas looked positively pained as he said this, and I liked him for not hiding the fact that he hated what he was doing.

"I can post bail," Verity began, and Luna and I both chimed in our assent.

"Ladies, save your money. This will all be sorted by Monday. I have faith our good chief of police here will find the real killer," Miss Elva said, positively relaxed for a woman who was being held for murder. The sex really must have been great, I thought, and then almost smacked myself in the forehead for thinking that as images flooded my head.

"Luna, Althea, you're both free to go. I'll get Miss Elva set up and see to her comfort. In the meantime, if you uncover anything…" At that, Chief Thomas pointed at his head. "You let me know. I'd be nothing but happy to have this resolved quickly."

"I think the first step needs to be seeing what more of the surveillance tape we can get," Luna said. "That would show how he left his room or if more people came in."

"I already asked for it. Problem is that it feeds to a company that stores it in the cloud or something. They aren't available until morning, so we're waiting."

"Then we need to try and track this anonymous email," I said.

"Also have IT on it. Which happens to be my college kid, who's studying forensics. I'll take help there as well. You know we're a small operation here," Chief Thomas sighed.

"Got it. We'll do what we can. You be nice to Miss Elva," I ordered.

Luna and I both hugged Miss Elva and made a move to go. Verity waved us out.

"I'll just stay and make sure my client's needs are being met before I go," Verity said, looking like she'd beat the crap out of Chief Thomas if he violated so much as a single right of Miss Elva's.

I knew I liked that woman.

Chapter Twenty-Two

WE SAT in Luna's car for a minute, just to catch our breath and to process everything we'd just learned. And it was a lot to process.

"So…" Luna began.

I just shook my head, scrubbing my hands over my face for a moment.

"I can't get images of Miss Elva…" I trailed off as I couldn't even say it.

"Let's not go there. But how about her choice in men? I didn't think Dominick was that great – and then to find out it's happened more than once? And what about the fact that she didn't bother to even say anything to us about knowing him?" Luna said, starting the car and pulling it to the automatic gate at the exit of the lot. Cars lined the street outside and I knew the reporters were waiting. Trace had already texted me that he was going back to my house to hang out with Hank until I got home – there were too many reporters for his liking.

I didn't blame him. The man ran a business here and I

could completely understand why he'd want to keep a low profile when such negative headlines were making the rounds.

"Yeah, she sure does keep her secrets close. Though in this case, I wonder if it was for protection. She certainly wasn't all that fussed when Chief Thomas showed up, so maybe she didn't tell us because the less we know, the better?"

Luna eased the car through the gate and flash bulbs went off. I blinked against them, holding my hand up, and Luna swore. The indelicate words coming from her delicate mouth made me want to smile.

"How can famous people drive through reporters like this? Honestly, I'll be lucky if I don't run one of them over," Luna griped.

"Please don't. The last thing we need is another dead body on our hands," I said.

"It would be their fault, not mine. Do you see how they're just jumping in front of the car? Who jumps in front of a moving car? Have they all lost their damn minds?"

"I wonder how much they get paid for photos. It has to be lucrative if they're throwing themselves in front of cars," I said as we finally left them behind and zipped toward my house.

"I'm just going to drop you off. I don't know what else to do tonight and I need some rest if we're going to run that spell tomorrow," Luna said.

I gaped at her. "We're going to do the spell without Miss Elva?"

"Um, yes. Althea Rose, in case you've forgotten, I do

happen to be a practitioner of magick," Luna said, rolling her eyes at me.

"I know that. It's just that… well, you know." I shrugged, annoyed with myself. "I'm not that great at magick yet and have a tendency to screw things up."

"Well, don't screw it up and you'll be fine," Luna said as she pulled to a stop in front of my house. The lights glowed from behind the shutters, which Trace had pulled closed for privacy.

"Easy for you to say," I said and sighed, twirling a lock of hair around my finger. "You're so confident at everything. I just fumble my way through with the magick stuff."

"Stop fumbling then," Luna said, as cranky as I'd seen her in a long time. "You have a lot more power than you're bothering to use or look into. Use it. Embrace it. Own it and learn how to wield it. It's like driving a stick shift. Scary at first, but once you get the hang of it, you own it. Stop running from this and make it happen. We need to figure out what happened to Dominick. Because – in case you forgot – his body was dropped at *your* shop, the killer is still loose, and someone clearly has their sights set on you. So stop your whining, put your big girl pants on, and start taking your magick seriously."

My eyes were probably the size of half-dollars by the time Luna had finished with her come-to-Jesus speech. It wasn't often that I had my butt kicked like that by my best friend, but it was definitely worth it when she did it. Luna was absolutely right – whining about something that made me uncomfortable would get us nowhere.

"You're right, Coach. Thanks for the talk." I leaned

over and hugged her, determined to not wimp out tomorrow and disappoint her.

"I love you. Go snuggle your dog and your man and get some rest. We've got to catch a killer."

"Yes, ma'am," I said.

At the very least, those were two orders I wouldn't screw up.

Chapter Twenty-Three

MY HEAD WAS THROBBING by the time I got inside – between the stress of my day, a touch too much tequila, and Miss Elva being thrown in jail, I was ready to curl up in a ball and pet my dog and pretend like the only care I had in the world was which dress to wear tomorrow.

Trace rounded the kitchen counter, where he was unpacking bags of Chinese takeaway, a loose long-sleeve shirt rolled to his elbows, his skin tanned from days on the water, and his hair left loose to curl softly around his ears. His eyes crinkled at the corners as he smiled at me and Hank danced after him, both the men in my life happy to see me.

It couldn't get better than this, right? Walking in the door after a tough day to a smiling man and a happy puppy. I should be grateful for the now and worry about the rest of it later, I thought, automatically wrapping my arms around Trace as he pulled me in for a hug and a nuzzle. I inhaled his scent – soap mixed with sea salt – and wrapped my arms more tightly around him. It was still new to me – being close like this – and I was feeling it out in my mind, and my heart, testing how it felt to come home to him in my kitchen with food waiting.

Or the fact that he had his own key.

Not like that had been a huge deal – several of my friends had keys to my house. We all looked after each other's places or checked up on each other's pets when one of us traveled, but still, the giving of a key always signifies something major in a relationship, in my opinion.

"Rough day?" Trace asked. I nodded, still holding onto him, my face buried into his neck for a moment. His hand traced lazy circles on my back and I was instantly both soothed and aroused.

"It was one for the books, that's for sure," I said.

"Want to tell me about it? I brought take-out."

"Ohhh, second dinner. My favorite," I said, laughing up at him. He dropped a kiss on my lips, which still sent little zings of excitement through me whenever his lips met mine.

"Inside or outside?"

"Inside," I decided. I just wanted to curl up on the couch – or even better, in bed – and let my mind check out. In a matter of moments we'd brought the cartons of food over to the couch, and I leaned into Trace as we both picked through boxes of rice and veggies.

"Tell me everything," Trace said, and so I did, starting with the craziness of my morning, all the way through Murray's ridiculousness, up until Miss Elva's arrest and her subsequent revelation that she'd been with Dominick the night before. By the time I'd finished, Trace had drained his beer, finished a carton of noodles, and started on a second beer, and was eying my half-eaten carton of fried rice. I offered it to him and he took it with a smile.

"You sure? I know a tough day equals comfort food."

"Yes – plus it looks like you need the comfort food, after hearing everything I just told you," I said. I felt a trickle of unease that he would throw a fit like Cash used to whenever he discovered I had once again gotten involved in something dangerous. Although, to be fair, I didn't get myself involved in anything this time. It had quite literally landed at my doorstep.

"Well, if you're going to ask me if I'm chill with you finding dead people in your office and hearing that some guy tried to tackle you in the parking lot of your store – no, I'm not. I'm not chill with it at all. It makes me angry and unhappy that I wasn't there to protect you or shield you from harm and having to see that. But, I also know you're a strong person and you can handle yourself. However, in the future, if we could try and stay away from finding dead bodies, that'd be great," Trace said, forking some rice into his mouth.

He'd been diving with me when we'd discovered a body a few months prior, and I knew he still had moments that it bothered him. Hell, I still woke up sometimes in a sweat thinking about having to lift the body from the water. Now with finding a body in my very own shop? I couldn't imagine I'd be sleeping well anytime soon.

"Yeah, I'd like to avoid that too. Thanks, though," I added, reaching up to pat his cheek.

"For what?"

"For not coming down on me for living a crazy life or getting involved in unusual situations," I said.

"Listen, Althea, just because Cash didn't approve of your life or whatever, that doesn't mean I have a problem with it, other than you putting yourself in danger. We've been friends for a long time and I've known you for even longer. You're cool with me."

Maybe it could just be as simple as that, I thought, snuggling deeper into the couch cushions. Maybe it was just finding someone who accepted you for you. Or, as Trace put it, someone you were cool with.

"How was your day?" I asked, realizing I'd been talking the entire time and hadn't caught up with Trace's day – though in all fairness, I did have the more dramatic story of the day to tell.

"It was fine. Weird, I guess," Trace shrugged and held up the fortune cookies for me to choose my cookie. We wouldn't want to pick each other's fortune, as that could be bad luck.

"How so?" I said, unwrapping the plastic on my cookie. Hank's ears appeared and then his nose followed, sniffing the air around my cookie.

"I had a sign-up for an open water course – a solo diver. But she honestly didn't seem that interested in learning. Asked a lot of questions about the town, about you, all my friends, and then proceeded to try and push this reality show on me. It was like, why even sign up for a course if you're not going to try and learn? Couldn't she have just, I don't know, cornered me at Lucky's or something? Instead I was stuck out on the boat with her all afternoon after her coursework this morning, and she just pushed and pushed this show."

"Cate," I said, finding myself unaccountably angry and

yet somewhat admiring of the fact that she hadn't taken my no for an answer in regard to the show. I had to admire a woman with tenacity, but this was really getting out of hand.

"I'm sorry." I met Trace's eyes. "That was a waste of your day and it's because of me. I told her yesterday in no uncertain terms that I wasn't interested in doing the show."

"I know. She told me. She seems to think she'll change your mind. I told her it wasn't likely." Trace's sexy grin flashed white in his tanned face. "But she still tipped well, so it was no skin off my back to deal with her today. I even ended up getting her focused long enough to get through much of the course. But we'll see if she finishes it out or not."

"You really don't mind? That she came at you like that?"

Trace smiled at me again, pulling one of my curls before leaning back and stretching his long legs out on the table in front of the couch.

"It's customer service. If I whined about every annoying client I had to deal with, I'd be one cranky man. It's no big deal. I still get paid and she was smart enough to tip me well. If she didn't really want to learn to dive, that's on her."

I let out the breath I'd been holding and patted his knee.

"What's your fortune say?" I asked.

"You first," Trace said.

I unfolded the little slip of paper that had been tucked inside the cookie, Hank's eyes following my every move. I tossed him a corner of the cookie and he caught it mid-air, racing away across the room as if we'd try to take it back from him even though it was already halfway down his throat.

"Live in the now, for tomorrow isn't guaranteed," I read. Even though I knew the fortunes were silly, it still sent a shiver of unease through me.

"Very Zen of them," Trace commented, and read his. "You're about to make great strides."

I looked up at him and his eyes danced with laughter before he added the old joke of "in the bedroom" to the fortune and pulled me from the couch. I squealed as he scooped me up and dragged me upstairs to forget about the horrible day in the best way we knew how.

After all, my fortune *had* told me to live in the moment, hadn't it?

Chapter Twenty-Four

TRACE HAD SUCCEEDED in taking the edge off my day, and I'd slipped into a – thankfully – dreamless sleep. He'd awoken me with a kiss while it was still dark; he was taking out a morning charter and needed to get the boat ready with supplies. I missed our morning dives, as I hadn't been out in weeks, but it probably wouldn't be my smartest move to go out diving when a killer was on the loose.

Though hanging out at my house alone probably wasn't so bright either. It would probably be best if I got my butt out of bed and over to Luna's so at least we were a team. I wasn't looking forward to this so-called soul level reenactment spell we'd be performing tonight, and after Luna's speech last night, I needed to spend some time with her today practicing some of the basics of magick that often seemed to elude me in the moment.

Picking up my phone, I read a text message from Beau.

I sincerely hope you have a good reason for not informing me about Miss Elva going to jail.

I texted off a quick apology explaining that I'd all but collapsed when I'd come home. Close enough, but best friends forgave each other for these kinds of things.

Hurrying through my morning routine, I found myself keeping my phone close and even double-checking the locks on windows and whatnot. It wasn't that I was expecting harm or getting any visions that I was in danger, but frankly at this point of the whole adulting experiment, it was probably important for me to pay attention to those kinds of details.

I didn't want to be one of those girls in the scary movies who runs upstairs instead of outside or to safety when a bad guy breaks through a window or the front door. I never understood that. Why do they run upstairs? Then you'd have to jump from a window instead of just running out the back door. If you jump from the window and a killer follows you, wouldn't he just be able to overtake you since you'd be limping from a broken leg or sprained ankle or something? As much as I sought my bed when I needed comfort, it wasn't going to save me if a murderer came strolling through the front door.

Considering that, I looked down at Hank.

"Want to come with me today, buddy?" I'd probably lose my mind if I left him at home and he was hurt by some insane madman. It was one of those things I'd never be able to forgive myself for. When I held up Hank's harness, he zipped across the floor and danced from paw to paw, a wriggling ball of joy.

"I'll take that as an adamant yes," I said, sliding the harness over his head, then packed a small bag of water, toys, and poop bags for him. Sliding it over my shoulder, I debated whether to take my bike and have him run beside me – something he did love – but not knowing how long I'd be out today, I decided on driving for once. Plus, my car was much faster at getaways than my slow legs would ever be.

It turned out to be the wise choice anyway, as I discovered that the tires on my beach cruiser had been slashed. I'd locked it on my front porch as usual yesterday, but was now kicking myself for not just rolling it inside the house. Especially with all the pandemonium in my life. My tires were expensive funky whitewall tires with a pink stripe running the length of the tire and I wasn't sure if I was angrier at myself for not taking extra protection for my bike, or at the person who had done it.

"Hold on, buddy," I said down to a wiggling Hank, and unlocked my bike and rolled it inside on the flattened tires just to be safe. Anger burned low in my stomach at being targeted when I'd done nothing to deserve it. That was the definition of victim, I mused as I walked Hank down the block to where my car was parked. Being careful, I made a full circle of the car and reached out with my mental senses to try and gauge if there was anything amiss. Finding nothing, I loaded Hank into the back seat and got in. Hank immediately put his paws on the center console to be my co-pilot in navigating. A very important doggy task, mind you.

Luna had instructed me to meet her at Miss Elva's that morning. Pulling in front of the house, I was surprised – but grateful – to see that the reporters hadn't camped out on her stoop.

Rafe hovered morosely on the porch, where he floated

above the cushy rocking chair, his hat pulled low over his face. Miss Elva was very specific about her porch time and instead of making a comfortable space where friends could all sit, she had her throne – the rocking chair – and a single wooden chair with no cushions for visitors. The message was loud and clear, and those who tried to stay too long would inevitably have a bottom that fell asleep from the hard chair.

"Devil beast," Rafe said, almost mournfully, down at Hank wiggling beneath the chair. He made no effort to move and I tilted my head at him.

"Having a rough day, Rafe?" I asked, barely able to conceal my cheerfulness. I know it was petty of me, but the pirate had given me more than my fair share of grievances since I accidently brought him through the veil, and it pleased me to no end to see the wind taken out of his sails. I knew he and Miss Elva would be patched up again in no time, so I figured I might as well enjoy this moment while I could.

"Yeah," Rafe sulked, picking at a wrinkle in his pantaloons as he sighed and stared across the street, the picture of a moping man if I'd ever seen one. Well, and considering I was the only one who *could* see him, I probably shouldn't make it so obvious I was talking to someone, or any of the neighbors walking by would be convinced that I'd finally gone off my rocker.

Deciding to wait on Luna and forgoing the awful visitor's chair, I perched myself on the first step of Miss Elva's porch, and Hank came to sit next to me, leaning just slightly into me as he took in the world going by.

"Must be all those years of womanizing catching up to

you," I said cheerfully, looking out over the street. Anyone passing by would think I was having a chat with Hank – which come to think of it could also look crazy, but I think most animal people would get it. We all talked to our animals.

"I don't see what that has to do with anything," Rafe said stiffly.

"Well, you know, payback and all. You can't go around taking any woman you please and then getting mad when your woman does the same thing. We call that a double standard," I explained, leaning back on my hands and crossing my legs. Today's maxi dress was a simple grey and black striped one, nothing too fancy for errands day. I'd tossed my hair in a messy bun, pulled a dress over my head, and considered my look done for the day. Sometimes you just have to roll with what you've got working for you naturally. No time to primp when we had to catch a killer. Thinking about it, I slitted a glance at Rafe. "You didn't slash my bike tires, did you?"

"I'd be slashing a lot of things right now, like your throat, if I could get myself to pick up a knife. Seems like that particular power isn't working for me," Rafe all but growled.

I smiled. "There's the bloodthirsty pirate we know and love."

Rafe mumbled something that sounded suspiciously like "kiss my ass," but was wise enough not to say it louder. Even though he didn't really like me all that much, I was one of the few people who could actually see him and have a conversation with him. He'd be wise not to alienate me completely.

"Rafe, you have to know Miss Elva spends time with men once in a while. We all need physical intimacy… and she obviously can't have that with you. You'll need to love her just as she is, just like she loves you just as you are. But putting rules on her is not going to work," I said, deciding to try and be nice.

"I just wasn't expecting it. She seems so devoted," Rafe admitted, in the most vulnerable tone I'd ever heard from him.

"She is devoted. She chooses to keep you around when she's kept no other man around. Think about that," I pointed out. The silence drew out until I turned to see what was going on.

"Why, peasant, you've finally made a good point for once in your life," Rafe said, and I honestly immediately regretted being nice to him. "She does pick me. The other men are just secondary. I'm the main one. I can live with that."

I wanted to point out that Rafe was no longer living, but it seemed superfluous at that point, as his good spirits were restored and Luna was pulling her Mini to a stop at the curb.

"Great. Glad we've got that sorted and you can move past that little pity party you were just having. Time to get things figured out so we can rescue Miss Elva from jail," I said.

Rafe leapt up so that he teetered on the porch railing, one hand in the sky like an enraged Peter Pan. "I will set her free! Breaking into jails was one of my specialties." Rafe licked his lips in anticipation while Hank vibrated in excitement beneath him.

"If you can't pick up a knife, I highly doubt you can break any locks or extract Miss Elva from jail," I said, patting Hank's rump to make him sit until Luna reached us before I allowed him to run down the stairs to greet her.

"I shall concede your point, peasant," Rafe said, his nose in the air.

I rolled my eyes. "Great, glad you can do that. Let's go inside. I'm done talking to you," I grumbled.

"You really need more sex in your life. Have we discussed this? I feel like you are constantly cranky. In my day we'd give a cranky one extra loving and that would do the trick," Rafe said.

"Rafe, my sex life is none of your business. I should have let you keep crying about Miss Elva. Talk about being cranky," I said.

"Yup, definitely unloved. Which isn't surprising, with that attitude," Rafe said, and flitted right through the wall of the house, leaving me with no chance to reply.

"I swear to the goddess... one of these days," I murmured to Luna as she pulled out the key to unlock the door.

"I know, I know. I'm proud of you, though. This adulting thing is paying off." Luna patted my shoulder and I scowled as I walked through the front door.

Life was much easier when you could just say what you wanted.

Chapter Twenty-Five

"I REALLY DON'T THINK you ladies should be doing magick," Rafe said from his spot on the couch. Or, to be precise, where he hovered just above the couch, Hank pacing below him.

"I really don't think a pirate can advise on magical doings. Especially one who has tried his hand at magick and failed," Luna said. She was going through the false bottom of a fancy curio tucked in the corner of Miss Elva's living room. Every once in a while, she would pause and mutter something to herself as she'd scan another book and put it gently aside. I was sprawled on the floor next to her, idly paging through one of the books, continuing to be awed by the sheer depth of Miss Elva's knowledge.

"Hmpf," was all Rafe said in response.

"How come he doesn't sass you but he constantly sasses me?" I asked Luna, annoyed that she never got any of the lip that Rafe seemed to forever enjoy giving me.

"Because you're obviously the weak one," Rafe said.

I held up the book in my hand. "Oh look, a banishing

spell," I said, and Rafe snapped his mouth shut to look up at the ceiling instead while Luna chuckled.

"She's not the weak one, Rafe. You'd be surprised how much power Althea has. That's something we're still discovering and are going to test out today before we do the spell tonight."

"We are?" I gulped past the trepidation that rose in my throat. My friend's life was at stake. As was potentially mine. I needed to test myself and also help in any way I could.

"Yes, we are. I need you to work on your focus. You distract easily, which is how we ended up with Rafe to begin with. Plus, you need to work on your confidence. Having power is something you should be proud of, confident in, and not neglect. I think if you'd just channel it and learn to focus, we'd be able to get you up to speed with some of your magicks. I mean, you can focus when you give readings; one would think you'd be able to focus once you get to your own magick," Luna said, skimming another leather-bound book and putting it aside.

"I don't know how to feel it," I admitted to her.

She paused, wrinkling her brow in confusion and looking like an impertinent fairy. "What do you mean?"

"It's just that the few times I've done magick, the power comes from somewhere in me that I don't really know or understand. When I'm working with clients or trying to see a vision or guiding them with tarot – I know what that feels like. I know where that power sources from. But the magick stuff? I don't understand it and have never been taught how to channel it. It's easier for me to dismiss it than it is to try it out, because it scares me that

I'll harm someone or use it out of context. Especially if my temper gets kicking. What if I reach for magick or something when I'm mad?"

Luna leaned back on her heels and studied me carefully.

"Have you ever picked up a knife to harm someone when you're angry?"

"No," I admitted.

"Have you ever picked up a gun to harm someone when you're angry?"

"No," I said. I hate guns. I didn't like touching them, going to gun ranges, being around them – none of it. The simple fact was that they were a weapon that could cause irrevocable changes when used in a blind instance of anger. I knew gun enthusiasts liked to point out that anything could be used as a weapon in a moment of rage, but a gun was the easiest and most often used. I hated them. I felt like so many people who had used guns in a fit of anger, or had even accidently discharged them by mishandling them, must live their lives wondering 'what if?' What if they'd just gotten a better night's sleep or had talked it out? I didn't like the finality that guns presented. Period.

"Have you ever hit someone or kicked the dog in anger?" Luna asked.

"No," I said.

"Then what makes you think you'd use your magick on someone in anger? Don't you think you'd be even more careful with it because you know the potential to harm someone is there?" Luna asked.

"But that's the thing – that's why I don't own a switchblade or even mace. I'm careless and often think too fast, and I'm clumsy. You remember the mace bedspread incident, don't you?"

Luna's lips quirked.

"I do."

My mother had given me a cylinder of mace for protection, and in lieu of keeping it in my purse – because let's be honest here, I was not going to be fast enough or coordinated enough to pull that out and use it if I really needed it – I'd tucked it in my bedside drawer. The reasoning was that if someone broke in downstairs, I'd have time to get the mace out and protect myself and Hank. Instead, one day I'd been cleaning and had pulled open my drawer to toss out some receipts and tidy up. When I'd slammed it shut, somehow I'd caught the lever on the spray and had managed to spray my brand-new comforter with pepper spray.

Now, I don't know if you've been pepper-sprayed before, but holeeeee shiitake, was it awful. Even though it hadn't hit me, the room had immediately filled, and tears ran from my eyes as I rolled the comforter in a ball and raced from the house with it, tears streaming and coughing up a fit. The neighbors had been doing some renovation work, so I'd dumped the blanket in the dumpsters and prayed that no homeless person would take it and get coated with the spray.

And that pretty much summed up why I didn't carry weapons. I forgot about them, misplaced them, and ultimately the only one who got hurt using them was myself.

"So, you can see why I'd be nervous to introduce

magick to my toolkit," I said, shaking my head as I remembered racing from the house with my comforter.

"I'm not going to lie," Luna said, laughter dancing on her face. "That is one of my favorite stories of yours."

"I could not believe that I'd maced my own bedspread."

"Probably the most heat that bed had seen in a while," Rafe piped up from his corner, and I glared at him.

"Can I please just…"

"No," Luna said firmly. "We are not getting rid of Rafe unless Miss Elva orders it. So you'd better stay on her good side, Rafe."

"I can't stay on any side of her if she has all these men." Rafe was back to sulking, and Luna rolled her eyes at me. Men and their egos.

"Ah, perfect. Here's the book she wants us to use. First we're going out back to practice some magickal basics, then we'll need to gather our ingredients for tonight. We'll need to be careful to slip back into the shop without anyone noticing," Luna mused.

"Since it's technically disturbing a crime scene," I said.

"Well, not if we don't touch anything. But we'll need to be careful nonetheless."

"Speaking of careful, the tires on my bike were slashed," I told Luna.

She stopped to look at me. "And you're just telling me this now?"

"What can you do about it?" I crossed my arms over my chest and looked at her.

"It's all useful information. It means you're being targeted. We still don't know why."

"No, we don't. Maybe one of these magickal spells will give us all the answers we need," I grumbled.

Luna squinted at me. "Are you and Trace fighting?"

"I told you she needs more loving," Rafe crowed from his perch on the couch.

"Get 'em, Hank," I ordered and Rafe screeched as Hank leapt on the spot where Rafe hovered, then proceeded to chase a squealing Rafe around the room. Luna shook her head at me, but I just laughed.

"That will never get old to me."

Chapter Twenty-Six

LUNA INSTRUCTED me to go outside to Miss Elva's sheltered back yard. I had to hand it to her – she'd really made an awesome space back here. With a fence over six feet high, she was ensured complete privacy. But she'd added tall pots of palm trees and plants that added extra privacy past the top of the fence, then she'd strung fun little globe lights between all the trees. In a surprise move, she'd used some beautiful marble for the flooring and added a small koi pond. Large cushions and low-slung couches were tucked around, creating an oasis that begged for you to slip your flip-flops off and curl up with a good book.

For my purposes, I headed to the corner where a small altar stood, with plenty of magickal items. I knew Luna would want me to sit down there, so I wandered over, stopping to say hello to the fish, before I plopped down on a cushion by the altar and waited for Luna to join me.

I hadn't much thought about my magick of late – for the most part I'd tried to ignore it. We had only recently discovered that I carried more power than we'd expected, and while Luna was hot to teach me all I needed to know about the magick and spells and being a white witch, it was also important that I wanted to learn it. A part of me really wasn't all that interested, though another part whispered to me that it would be so very cool if I could do some sort of spell to help people in need. The problem was, there were so many rules and things to remember. I knew it was important that you didn't mess with someone's choices, as that could potentially disrupt their destiny. It was also important to analyze each spell and determine if the magick you were wielding could potentially cause harm. If so, it was best to avoid it or look for another solution. Because of the poor reputation witches had, it was even more important that they didn't wield magick that would harm or curse anyone. They already had years of stereotyping and myths to overcome.

It was because of all these things that I wasn't quite sure I was ready to sign up for the whole white witch crash course. But at the same time, Miss Elva needed us. Luna had been explicitly clear that it was *us*, not just her. For my friends, who had repeatedly put themselves on the line for me, I would do anything.

"Looks like we're all set for the necessary ingredients of the spell tonight," Luna said, coming out carrying the book in her hand. Hank wandered out after her, found himself a cushion, and plopped down away from us, seeming to know we needed space to work. Rafe peeked out the door, took one look at us sitting by the altar with magick books, and zipped back inside.

"Miss Elva does keep a well-stocked pantry," I said.

"First up, we need to work on you casting your circle

and protecting yourself. From there we'll work on how you call your power. It'll be the best we can do before the spell tonight. Remember, we need to protect you and your power, and then channel your power. Got it?"

"Yes, boss," I said, grinning at her.

She stuck her tongue out at me. "Let's get started. Do you remember how to cast a circle?" Luna asked, and I nodded, though I was already certain I would screw it up.

Luna slid me a glance and then sighed, leading me through the steps of casting a circle, taking her time to explain the elemental points and why a circle is considered protective. Using salt, she poured a circle around us and helped me work my way through the basic ritual. Once we'd run it, she asked me to pause and close my eyes.

"Do you feel it?"

I stood with my eyes closed and allowed myself to drop my shields so I could feel whatever it was she was trying to have me feel. Sure enough, I began to sense something almost like waves pulsing at me. In my mind's eye it was as though we were standing in a cylinder of calm, and outside of the cylinder, waves of energy pulsed and bounced off our protective sphere.

"It's almost like these waves of energy. It kind of feels like when you've been on a boat all day and close your eyes but it still feels like you're rocking," I murmured, keeping my eyes closed.

"That's a good way to describe it. And, much like the ocean, not everything is kind and gentle. Energy is a natural thing, but – as with anything in nature – there are predators. In our case, that would be the bad energy predators. We don't want to let demons or energy vampires sneak into our dealings and feed off our beautiful and pure energy that is meant to do good. So the circle is enacted to protect the work we are doing here. We are the lightworkers, do you understand?"

"Yes, now that I feel it more. Not that I doubted there was bad energy out there," I said, my eyes still closed. I'd seen some bad energy at work in recent months. However, even when you removed magick spells or extra-sensory abilities, you could still see bad energy at work in everyday normal people. The lightworkers were the ones who always looked on the bright side, the forever optimists, the ones whose presence felt like bathing in sunshine. I'd always admired those people; they drew people to them like bees to honey and seemed naturally charismatic. Now, I understood that they too were lightworkers, spreading little doses of kindness and light with every smile or good deed they did. The bad energy ones were constantly negative, and after an interaction with them it was as though all your energy was drained and a cloud followed over your head.

Ultimately, I thought, we all could practice magick daily, in our own ways – even if only through smiles or offering a word of kindness when we could. Magick doesn't have to be running spells or anything major. Sometimes the smallest doses make the biggest impact. As a very famous man once said, 'If you think you're too small to make a difference, just ask a mosquito.' I smiled to myself, almost humming in joy, and Luna snapped her fingers, causing me to pop my eyes open.

"Careful, girl, or you're going to get happy-drunk on the magick," Luna said, smiling at me.

"Is that what was going on? I swear I was ready to start handing out free hugs and skipping through fields of flowers while singing of my joy," I admitted, and she laughed.

"The light makes you feel good. It's easy to get a little tipsy on it. So long as you don't let it pull you in. As with anything, moderation is really the key. Too much of a good thing can ultimately be a bad thing. You'll become better at putting your boundaries up the further along we go. Now, let's work on focusing your magick and running a basic spell. In this spell, I'd like you to light the candles sitting in those dishes across the way." Luna pointed to several candles of varying sizes, cluttered on a small table near where Hank rested. Hank lifted his head at her gesture, and if a dog could look incredulous, he did.

"Maybe Hank should go inside for this," I said, suddenly nervous I'd shoot a fireball at my adorable dog.

Luna considered that for a moment and then, muttering a protective spell under her breath, she stepped from the circle and took Hank inside – much to Rafe's disdain, I'm sure – and came back out. It was interesting to note that I could feel her enter and leave the circle, almost like suction pulling the energy out.

"Okay, no more excuses. Let's try this. First, I need you to close your eyes again and find your power within you."

"Um, like how exactly?" It was like when a life coach tells you to find your purpose in life and you'll be happy. Much easier said than done. Like you were just supposed to wake up one day and decide that you've always wanted to write poetry for a living and suddenly you'd be happy. It was never as easy as it sounded.

"We're lightworkers. Close your eyes and look for the light. Where is it inside of you? Find it in your mind's eye, hold it, blow on it like a flame or a coal in a fire until it warms you. Once you feel warm, send your energy – gently – to the candles over there."

That didn't sound too difficult. Closing my eyes once again, I took a few deep breaths and tried to center myself, like they tell you to in yoga.

Who was I kidding? I went to yoga like once a year.

Batting those thoughts away, I breathed slowly until I began to feel calmer, and started trying to imagine where the light in me would be. Eventually, a small pinprick of light, the tiniest little golf ball of light, seemed to radiate from my core. I focused in on it until I felt it begin to flood through me. So this is what my power is, I thought, and smiled. Feeling confident, I pictured the candles across the way and sent my energy to them.

"Althea!" Luna's sharp response made my eyes pop open.

The candles were incinerated, nothing but melted piles of wax, while the cushions where Hank had been sleeping were currently burning merrily. I gasped, bringing my hands to my face while Luna worked quickly with her magick to douse the flames.

"I'm sorry, I'm sorry, I'm sorry," I said, torn between horror at what I could have done to my dog and an almost hysterical blip of laughter that threatened to work its way out.

"Gently. Very gently. The tiniest whisper of energy,"

Luna said calmly, running her hand down my arm to soothe me. "You are more powerful than you realize. That was like an eight on the power scale. Let's bring it down to a one, okay?"

I nodded, but felt nervous about continuing. Stalling, I opened my mouth to speak, but Luna cut me off.

"I'm going to make you keep doing this until you've got it more under control. So deal with it, and I'll deal with the wrath of Miss Elva if you destroy her yard."

"Great, now I have the image of destroying her yard in my head," I said, crossing my arms over my chest and feeling the familiar crankiness flood me at being forced to do something I didn't want to do.

"Remember, this is all for the greater good. Your power feels good. It's meant to be used for good. It's all a circle of good and light. Just breathe through it." Luna's voice was hypnotic as she soothed me back down and I refocused on the ball of light.

I'm not sure how long we worked the spell for, but – finally! – I was able to light new candles with no collateral damage. Granted, the flames may have shot a little higher than necessary when being lit, but after destroying a few more of Miss Elva's cushions, I'd take it.

"Whoop! I did it!" I laughed, and Luna high-fived me.

"Once more," she instructed.

I grumbled. I'd thought I was done for now. I really wanted a donut as a reward for my hard work. "Fine," I said, and began working the spell again.

Just as I was about to finish it, Rafe popped into the circle, distracting me.

"You wenches had better not burn the house down. It's like a war zone back here," Rafe said, glaring at me.

"Rafe! No!" Luna shouted at him for breaking our circle. We both gasped when a hazy apparition flitted past us – neither of us more shocked than Rafe – and Luna hastily closed the circle.

"What the…" I gasped.

We all turned, Rafe included, to stare at the apparition hovering before us. A lusty wench if I'd ever seen one, with massive cleavage, a tumble of curls, and a low-cut bodice with a corset to push her ladies high – she looked like one of those sexy pirate wench Halloween costumes come to life.

Er, ghost, that is.

"Rosita," Rafe breathed.

Uh-oh.

Chapter Twenty-Seven

"WELL, WELL, WELL," Rosita said, tossing her curls back over her shoulder and putting a hand on her hip. Her upper lip curled in disgust when she saw Rafe. "Look what the cat dragged in. Still looking for love, Rafe?"

"I didn't bring you here, Rosita," Rafe exclaimed, pointing back to where we stood gaping at her. "These peasants did."

Rosita floated over to examine us, her perusal languid, and by the end of it I felt like I'd been violated by her look alone. Crossing my arms over my chest, I glared at her. She threw her head back and laughed, curls and bosom bouncing alike.

"Oh, I like this one. She's got spirit. And that hair – the color of the sea at sunset? Yes, I'd know several clients who'd like a romp with her," Rosita mused.

Excuse me?

"How do you know Rafe?" I asked sweetly, dying to get the goods on him while I had someone else from his time period here.

"Don't!" Rafe began, but Rosita shut him up with one look.

"I'm the madam of the most popular brothel in a port that shall not be named. Rafe was a regular. Seems he had trouble finding love, and, like every man, needed the comfort of a woman at times," Rosita said, shrugging. The hard edges of her time and job showed through in the lines on her face and the directness of her words.

"Well, isn't that interesting," I murmured. "Rafe, I had no idea you were such a softie. I thought you were out plundering the seven seas and taking women as prisoners left and right."

"I was a damn good pirate. People feared my name and ran when my ship came to port," Rafe insisted, but Rosita threw back her head and laughed that hearty laugh once more.

"Not quite as he says – but, well, a man's ego and all. It's probably best I don't enlighten you ladies to his real reputation. I've kept many a man's secrets, and will continue to do so."

Now I was dying of curiosity, but Luna had other questions.

"How did you manage to get through the veil?" Luna asked.

Rosita shrugged. "I'm not sure. I saw this… like a light, and all these fireworks going off. I've always loved a good fireworks show, so I came over to see what was going on. Then, I kind of just glimpsed a hole – sort of a porthole, perhaps? – for a second. And I ducked my head through to get a better look and, well, here I am," Rosita looked around. "Though it is hard to say where, exactly."

"You should go home," Rafe grumbled.

"Home is relative once you're dead, isn't it? This looks like a lot more fun."

Lovely, another ghost that was going to be sticking around, I thought, and met Luna's eyes.

"You've really got to work on staying focused, Althea. We can't have portholes opening to the otherworld," Luna pointed out.

I felt my lip poke out in a pout. "Listen up, you're the one who wanted me to do this. I told you I'd be bad at it. Didn't I warn you? Maybe it's best to just let my power rest. I can't have the threat of opening doors to other worlds and burning down patios hanging over my head. None of that's an issue when I'm reading tarot cards and getting visions of the future. I was happy just doing that. Why doesn't anyone believe me when I say I'm content with my life as is?" I'd begun to pace the backyard and Rosita followed along at my shoulder, seeming highly interested in every word I was saying.

"You're a seer, is it? Ah, another woman with an unusual job. Us women who live life outside the normal way of doing things should stick together," Rosita said. "Have you ever considered working at a brothel?"

I sputtered and shook my head, and it was now Rafe's turn to throw back his head and laugh.

"This one could certainly use it. She's very angry these days," Rafe said, and Rosita eyed me wisely.

"Ah, some time between the sheets would cure that."

"I don't think she likes the pleasures of the flesh. Look how uptight she is," Rafe interjected before I could speak.

I whirled to glare at him. "Rafe, my sex life is none of

your business. I've told you that repeatedly. And I am certainly not sexless. I just choose not to share it with you. You're the only one around here not having sex. Or need I remind you of where Miss Elva was last night?"

Okay, so that was mean. When Rafe gave me a look like a puppy that had just been kicked, then floated inside, I briefly considered apologizing.

"Don't let his sulking bother you in the least, honey," Rosita said from over my shoulder. "He was one of the clients I had to baby more. Sometimes men just need their hand held. I swear, half the time my women spent with him was just listening to him talk, stroking his ego in lieu of stroking his –"

Luna and I both interrupted her before she could go any further.

"We got it, we got it," Luna said.

"I like you two. Maybe not as bawdy as the girls I usually spend time with, but you'll do," Rosita decided. "Why don't you show me around your town?"

Luna and I both turned to look at each other.

"Well, we're not exactly sight-seeing today," Luna said.

"That's fine. Just bring me along with you wherever. There seems to be so much to learn about this time," Rosita said, her intelligent eyes alight with curiosity. The screen door banged open and Hank burst out, having exhausted his ability to wait inside.

"Oh!" Rosita exclaimed and I waited for Hank to chase her around the patio. Instead, he sat immediately and looked up at her, all but drooling in adoration.

"He is yours?" Rosita whispered at my ear, and I

nodded. She looked down at him, then floated closer so that they were almost touching. Hank tried to lick her face and then looked confused when nothing happened. Rosita tossed her hair and laughed, real delight suffusing her face this time. "What an absolute doll baby. I've always wanted a dog, but it didn't make sense in my line of work. Too many distractions, and a lot of men don't like dogs for some reason. This one seems quite charming. What's his name?"

"Hank," I said, warming to the ghost.

"Oh, hello Master Hank. You are just the sweetest, most handsome, smartest dog to ever roam this earth, aren't you?" Rosita cooed – and if you can believe it, my dog rolled right over and looked at the ghost like he'd fallen in love.

"See?" Rosita looked over her shoulder at me. "Stroke the man's ego and they'll fall for you every time."

I couldn't argue with her logic.

Chapter Twenty-Eight

IT APPEARED we had an entourage now, after determining that Rosita was along for the ride, and that Rafe was coming with as well – even though he didn't want to be around her, but he also was used to getting constant attention. Throw in an ecstatic Hank, who couldn't decide which ghost was more worthy of his attention, and we had a choice to make. We couldn't run the spell until nighttime; it wasn't smart to hang at my house; Luna's place was too nice to bring my dog to – think white everything – and I was starving.

Who had white couches anyway? Weren't they just asking for stains? Who were these people who could function wearing white clothes and having white couches and upholstery? Sure, I was trying the whole adulting thing, but I certainly wasn't adult enough to not spill wine or manage to keep my dog off the couch.

"Should we get food and just come back here?" I asked Luna as I opened the front door to leave.

"I don't think we're coming back here," Luna said. Her

words were soft, but her eyes shot a warning as she pointed over my shoulder. Turning, I found a voodoo doll pinned to the front door with a lethally sharp-looking dagger stabbed through its heart. Surprised to find that I was more angry than scared, I yanked the dagger out and tossed it in my purse.

"I'm not going to let some jerk terrorize us. We're going to get food and then we'll do the damn spell and catch us a killer," I declared.

Rosita nodded sagely at me from her perch on the couch where Hank drooled up at her. "That's my kind of woman. No need to faint at the sight of a wee knife," she commented.

"Okay, Wonder Woman, where are we going for food?" Luna asked.

I decided on the coffee shop for sandwiches and a caffeine boost. I certainly didn't want to bring any more drama to Lucky's, as Beau really needed to stay focused on his restaurant launch.

Twenty minutes later we were sitting on a bench by the water, reasoning that broad daylight in public was the safest spot to be if a mad killer was trying to overtake us. Luna had woven a protection spell around us, including the ghosts in it, so we had a sort of magickal cocoon that she swore would help us if anyone did come threaten us.

The sun was already dropping toward the horizon, which made me realize just how long we'd been practicing my magick for.

"I feel like we were kind of in a time warp. And I'm ravenous," I said, opening a package of dill-flavored potato chips.

"Working magick is hungry business. But it burns calories, as your metabolism is zipping along," Luna said, biting into a meatball sandwich. How this woman could eat something like a meatball sandwich while wearing white was beyond me.

"That could actually be enough to motivate me to practice it more," I mused, adding mustard to my turkey sandwich and spilling a drop on my maxi dress. See what I mean? I sighed and scrubbed the stain, happy to see it disappear quickly. "Burning calories without going to the gym would be a nice bonus."

"There are other, more... zesty ways to lose weight," Rosita declared.

I looked at her buxom figure and sighed. "Wear a corset daily?" I asked.

"No, that's just to entice the men. Though you do eat less when your stomach is restricted." Rosita shrugged like it was no big deal. I couldn't imagine being constrained like that every day.

"Who do you think the dagger belongs to?" Luna changed the subject, and we left Rosita to coo at Hank while Rafe hovered, casting looks of annoyance at all of us – as if we were all that happy to have him hanging out with us either.

"My gut says Murray. Though I'm not sure what the point of him doing this is. I know Miss Elva thinks he's in on it, but I just can't see him being a killer. I feel like he's irrational, highly tempestuous, and not as bright as Dominick was."

"Nice use of 'tempestuous,'" Luna observed.

I smiled, pleased with myself. "It's part of my more

adult vocabulary. I just wanted to test it out," I said, and Luna laughed.

"If it is Murray, what's his point? We already know he's mad at us. Why slash your tires or waste a nice knife to leave behind in someone's door?"

I pulled the knife out from my bag, where I'd tossed it before we left the house. I noted that it was now stuck through my change purse, and sighed. Have I mentioned that I'm not good with carrying weapons around?

"Perhaps I'll take that off your hands," Luna said, gingerly taking the intricate knife from my hands and examining it. With a carved wooden handle and a wicked looking blade, it was clearly meant to do some damage.

"It looks like it means business," I said, and Luna agreed.

"It's a ritual knife," she said, and held it up so that the blade glinted in the sun before slipping it into a side pocket of her bag.

My phone rang – a number I didn't recognize – and I answered. It wasn't something I would typically do, but hey – psycho-killer and friend-in-jail kind of day.

"Hello?"

"It's Chief Thomas. This is my private number. Miss Elva is insisting that I give it to you. Are you two up to something I need to be aware of?" The chief sounded tired, harassed, and like he needed a good meal.

"Um," I said, "at the moment, no. Just eating a sandwich by the water."

"Keep your phone on you. And next time call me before you do anything stupid. Understood?" He hung up without saying goodbye.

I programmed his phone number into my speed dial and gave it to Luna as well.

"It doesn't hurt to have it," she reasoned.

"It's not like this will be the last time we need it, if the last six months are any indication of how much our lives have changed," I said.

"Think it'll stay this way? I miss our easy-going days," Luna admitted and leaned in a bit to bump me with her shoulder. We watched as the sun sank lower on the horizon, spreading its crimson rays over the water in a fiery display that I hoped wasn't a premonition for our future.

"I think change is inevitable. Let's just hope that the next change will bring us more good than bad," I murmured.

"Bad things happen. The only thing you can control is how you respond," Rosita piped up, a shimmering harlot full of wisdom nodding wisely on the bench. I suppose she had some experience, having been dead for a couple hundred years, and had seen more than I had.

"That's the truth of it, then. Time to take charge and catch ourselves a killer," I said. I stood and tossed my trash in the garbage can, my eyes scanning the parking lot behind us for any signs of danger.

"Have I mentioned that I have a growing fondness for you? Some men like those take-charge women. You'd really do well in a brothel. Do you tie people up?" Rosita asked, and Luna shot me a grin.

"Sure, Rosita." I rolled my eyes. "I'll tie people up. Whatever you think is best…"

Chapter Twenty-Nine

IT WAS full dark when we arrived at the shop, having collected everything we'd need for the spells from Miss Elva's house, then driving around a bit to make sure nobody was tailing us. Not that I had much experience in spotting a tail, but Luna was far more observant and suspicious than I. Hank bounced back and forth on the back seat, about as happy as a dog could be, and Rosita cooed sweet nothings to him while Rafe sulked in the corner. Overall, I felt like we were a ragtag band of do-gooders who would hopefully set things to right.

And, you know, not get ourselves killed or maimed in the process.

My heart leapt into my throat when the headlights flashed across the front of our shop, and Luna gripped my arm.

"Oh no," she whispered. "Turn your lights off."

I flicked my headlights off and did my best to control the rage that threatened to boil up in my throat. We'd put a lot of blood, sweat, and tears into our place of business. To have it violated twice in a week was devastating.

The word MURDERERS had been viciously spray-painted across the walls of the front porch, each letter taller than I was. The blood red of the spray paint stood out starkly against the walls of our chic cottage shop. Police tape ordering passersby not to cross fluttered in the breeze. The light of the rising full moon gleaming off the bright yellow made them seem like some macabre party streamers.

"It's just paint, right? We can paint again. We've talked about changing up the color anyway," I said, easing the car slowly around the side of the shop, the wheels crunching against the gravel, but not another sound to be heard.

"It's just… it feels so violating. All we do is try and help people," Luna murmured, and I could feel her pain.

"I know. We've built something beautiful here and we do spend our days helping others and trying to make their lives better. We don't deserve this, nor does our pretty little shop," I agreed, turning the car off. We stared at the cottage in silence for a moment, the light of the full moon easily illuminating the lot, and let ourselves process the emotions.

"It's fine. We'll handle this. Paint is paint. I've picked up some new colors anyway. I'm thinking maybe a faded teal… almost a weathered blue or grey, maybe with maroon trim? Just to shake things up a bit and give it a fresh look?" Luna asked briskly, and I saw her slip the knife from her purse. Smart woman.

"Sure, Luna. That would be lovely. I think it'd be fun to give it a bit of a facelift. Maybe we can put a little porch swing up or something too." I chattered on, trying to ease the tension with my words, until I saw Luna blow out a breath and nod. It was more important that she be on point and controlled, as she was going to be the one channeling all the magick tonight. In all likelihood, I was probably still a loose cannon, so we needed Luna to stay focused.

"I like decorating. This could be fun," Luna decided, and I smiled at her.

"Cheeky wenches. Love your spine, ladies," Rosita announced from the backseat.

I smiled. There was something about having a madam from the olden days give us some kudos that made me proud. Goddess knows she'd probably seen and handled some really tough stuff, so it sort of felt like a badge of honor to gain her approval.

"Let's just hope the shop isn't damaged," Luna said.

"We'll go take a look. Come on, Hank," I ordered. Not that I was excited to bring him into any potential danger with me, but I'd rather have him by my side than stuck in a car if a crazy person decided to make their next point by harming my dog.

Gingerly, we tried the back door to Luna's side of the shop. I was happy to see that it was still locked, with no damage to the door. Luna unlocked it and ordered everyone inside swiftly, where darkness met us. Flicking her hand at a candle, she illuminated it with a skill that took my breath for a moment. Even after years of seeing Luna do magick, and even knowing that I now could do the same, it never ceased to amaze. I wasn't entirely sure if I ever wanted it to, either. There was something so beautiful and amazing about a power such as hers or even mine, and I would hate to become jaded or unappreciative of its sheer awesomeness.

We eased the door to the shop open and peeked out. The security lights that softly illuminated the room didn't show anything amiss.

"Seems clear?" I asked Luna, my voice a whisper.

"Yes. Let's go to your shop. Let me get the supplies," Luna said. She stepped back outside to go to the car for our supplies, and a feeling of dread filled me.

"Luna, wait," I whisper-yelled. It was when Hank growled, low and ugly in his throat, that fear laced my stomach.

Luna backed her way into the shop, her hands up, the dagger she'd been carrying now at her throat as a shaking Murray glared at me. He gestured wildly toward Hank, whose growling had grown louder.

"Shut that dog up," Murray ordered.

"Hank, come here, buddy," I ordered. When he did, I eased him behind me into the shop and shut the door. I knew he'd be worked up that I was keeping him from the action, but I wanted him out of danger.

Murray's brow was coated in a sheen of sweat and the whites of his eyes showed, like a horse terrified and about to buck. I kept my eyes trained on the hand with the knife, which was shaking.

"Murray, you don't have to do this," I said softly, easing myself away from the door and toward one of Luna's shelves – hoping to find a weapon of sorts.

"Of course I have to do this. Dominick was one of my best friends. If you thought I wouldn't avenge his death, you're dead wrong. Ha," Murray laughed a little as he swayed, "dead wrong. Get it? A soul for a soul. Or two souls for one. Because that's what Dominick was – larger than life. And you stole that from him. Snuffed it out. For no reason." Murray ground the words out and I tensed as he moved the knife closer to Luna's throat.

"It doesn't work like that, Murray," I said as calmly as I could, though reasoning with crazy was virtually impossible. "You don't trade soul for soul. There is no cosmic ledger sheet out there where you balance the books out. Plus, it would only add to your deficit, as Luna and I weren't the ones to kill Dominick. That's what we're doing here tonight, by the way, trying to find the real killer," I explained, feeling behind me in the dark, hoping to find a weapon of any sort.

"Lies," Murray spat, the knife wavering. "Nothing but lies. He was dead in *your* shop. You were the last to see him."

I saw Luna trying to mouth something at me but didn't want to take my eyes away from where the knife waved by her throat.

"That's actually not true. Miss Elva was," I said, and heard Rafe begin swearing behind me as I brought up that little reminder again. Couldn't the ghost keep quiet for once in his life? It wasn't all about him all the time.

"Miss Elva saw him? She killed him?" Murray asked, his eyes wide in confusion. The knife dropped just as I realized what Luna was saying. She'd been mouthing 'fire' at me. I closed my eyes to breathe and try to center myself, searching deep within for that little ball of light. Finding it was easier this time, and I made a promise to myself that if

I hurt Luna or burned the shop down, then I was retiring from magick and moving across the world.

Opening my eyes, I looked at Murray and said, "No, she didn't kill him either. If you'd listen, we are trying to help you. We're on your side. The last thing we want is to deal with murderers, dead bodies, or – least of all – psycho knife-wielding half-assed assistants," I said.

When Murray's mouth dropped open in rage, I flicked a wave of magick at the hand holding the knife. He squealed in terror, dropping the knife as he grabbed his hand and shrieked.

"You burned me! How did you…"

His words trailed off as he slumped to the floor, a satisfied Luna standing over him with a potted plant in her hand.

"Let's tie him up. He may actually be helpful in the recreation," Luna said, then smiled brightly at me. "Great job on the magick. I'll take that as a pat on the back for me being an awesome teacher, because for a moment there I was convinced you were going to incinerate us both."

"I was just as worried," I admitted, letting out the breath I'd been holding.

"See? Stronger than you realized," Luna almost sang.

I had to admit it felt good not to screw something up for once.

Chapter Thirty

WE WERE all assembled in my office, which, luckily Murray had decided not to destroy when he'd vandalized the front of the cottage. I pulled my blackout shades and lit a small skull lamp that I had in the corner. A warm glow washed softly over the room.

Murray had come to shortly after, but we'd already restrained him and given him a light sedative – it didn't hurt that Luna had all the ingredients necessary for that type of thing in her workshop – and had forced him at knifepoint to come into my shop, where he now sat on the floor with his back against the wall and his legs straight out in front of him.

"So this is it, then? This is how it ends?" Murray whispered, almost to himself, his head hung low.

"No, Murray. This is not how it ends. Do you or do you not want to find out what happened to Dominick? For the last time, we did not hurt your friend," Luna said, her voice shockingly stern for her. I certainly didn't blame her; I would be a little testy too after having a knife held to my throat. But her tone seemed to register with Murray, and he sat up a little straighter.

"You really didn't?" His voice all but squeaked.

"We really and truly didn't, Murray. Frankly, I would have murdered you long before Dominick if I were the murdering type," I said, annoyed that this little eejit did not seem interested in hearing us.

"Then who?" Murray demanded. "Who else was his enemy? He was so well-liked."

"I'm wondering if it isn't maybe you," Luna began, and Murray had the nerve to look shocked.

"Me? Why me?"

"Because this could all be a show. We heard word that you wanted the TV show for yourself. Maybe you thought getting rid of Dominick would not only add drama to the reality show headlines, but would also pave the way for you to have your own TV career?" Luna said.

Murray's mouth gaped open like a big-mouth bass before he snapped it shut. "I'm not going to pretend I didn't want to be on that show. But with him, not without him. I'm... stronger with him," Murray admitted. He yawned, the sedative clearly relaxing him.

"But maybe you'd have liked it if you were the head-liner?" I asked, crossing my arms over my chest and leaning back on my desk to survey him.

"I wanted equal billing, that's all. I'm sick of always being the assistant. And I made sure Cate knew that, in no uncertain terms," Murray said, his eyes drooping a bit as he struggled to stay awake.

"How much of that stuff did you give him?" I asked Luna.

"Enough to make sure he wasn't a flight risk is all," she said. We both watched as Murray's breathing slowed and then came out in even little puffs of air, indicating he'd slipped over into dreamland. Hank went over and sniffed him, and I swear I could see my dog actually consider lifting a leg to pee on Murray.

"Hank, no," I laughed. I couldn't help it. Hank looked at me as if to say, 'come on, mom!' But I shook my head and pointed to the bed I had for him in the corner. He went and curled up, but stayed alert. I think after the threat of earlier, he wasn't quite ready to slip off into sleep.

"So are we going to do this spell with him right here?" I asked, nodding at Murray.

Luna shrugged. "I suppose if he does have any psychic ability he should be able to see what we see and then know it wasn't us," she said.

"But he's sleeping."

"That'll wear off by the time we do the reenactment. Don't forget, we first have to find Dominick and talk to him to get his agreement before we can even start the re-enactment."

"Another spell? I'm out," Rafe said, and Rosita wisely ducked out after him. I think she was enjoying this side of the veil and I suspected we'd have just as much difficulty sending her back as we did with Rafe. But that was a problem for another day.

"What's the plan? How do I do a circle here? Do we need one? Where's the salt?" Wasn't I the chatty one all of a sudden?

"Althea, calm down. It's fine. We'll call the circle, and run the spell to see if we can find Dominick to start.

Nothing bad will happen, I promise," Luna soothed, though I think she could understand why I was nervous. I mean, how many ghosts did I need to bring through the veil? Before too long I wouldn't be able to get any work done with ghosts chattering in my ear all day. Then I'd become Old Crazy Althea who mutters to herself, and people would steer a wide berth around me on the streets. I already had a bad enough reputation in this town; it was best not to make it worse. Though I didn't think I could get much lower than I was now, what with the recent news headlines. But, hey, I'm nothing if not an overachiever. I'm sure I could really hit the bottom of the barrel if I tried.

Luna pulled a little jar of pink salt from her bag and sprinkled it in a circle in front of my desk. For a moment I wanted to be annoyed; then I remembered that a man had died here today. I was going to be cleaning the entire office – floor to ceiling. A little salt wasn't going to change that.

Letting Luna take the lead on this one – not like I was about to take charge – I chanted when she told me to, closed my eyes and called on my power when instructed, and when I opened them… nothing had happened.

"So…"

"Shh, just wait. We've called him over from the other realm. Give him a little time, would you?" Luna murmured, her gaze focused in the soft light in my office.

Minutes passed and I began to grow antsy, shifting from foot to foot – patience wasn't exactly my strong suit. Looking down, I fidgeted with my watch and was beginning to open my mouth to ask a question when Luna tapped me. When I looked up, I gasped. Dominick stood before us, almost as real as life, except I could faintly see Murray through him where the light was shining.

He looked confused, somewhat disheveled if a ghost can be disheveled, and very angry.

"I demand to know what's going on here," Dominick said, his strong voice booming out and startling Murray from his sleep.

"Is that you, Dom?" Murray said softly.

Dominick whirled, looking down at his assistant, who lay tied up on our floor. "You'd better explain yourselves immediately. What have you done with Murray? And did you drug me? I just don't…" Dominick looked down at his hands, confused. "I don't remember. Where I've been or what… it's all just cloudy. And weird. I feel like my brain is slogging through mud."

Luna's eyes met mine, and I shook my head in shock. This was beyond anything I knew how to handle.

Because – if I was reading this correctly – Dominick didn't know he was dead.

Chapter Thirty-One

"I ASKED, WHAT. IS. HAPPENING!" Dominick almost roared.

I jumped back as he tried to take a step forward but was met with resistance from our circle of protection. Okay, this was the last time I was going to give Luna a hard time about casting a circle. She was right: They were a necessary component when you were dealing in any kinds of magick. I wasn't entirely sure what an angry spirit who didn't know he was dead could do to us, but I also wasn't interested in finding out the answer to that. All I really wanted to do was wrap this up so I could go back to watching trash television on my sofa and reading my clients during the day. What had happened to my easy life?

"Dominick, do you know where you are?" Luna asked carefully. I let her lead, because knowing me I'd say something snarky and get us in trouble.

"I'm in Althea Rose's office," Dominick said automatically. At least that was good, as his brain didn't seem to be damaged, I thought.

"You are partially correct," Luna said, again picking her words carefully.

"What do you mean, 'partially'? And what have you done with Murray?" Dominick pointed down to where Murray goggled up at him, the sedative still making his response time slow.

Luna drew in a deep breath and looked at me. I, in turn, looked at Dominick. Unlike Luna, I knew the look of a man about to blow. People got mad at me much more easily than they did Luna. Probably because she didn't use sarcasm as liberally as I did.

"Dominick, I have some bad news for you. I don't know how else to say this, so I'm just going to rip the Band-Aid off," I said, hoping I was reading him right. "But, you're dead."

"I'm… what?" Dominick laughed, paused, and then threw back his head and laughed again. We didn't say anything, just waited it out. It was probably best to let him come to terms with it in his own time. "Come on, ladies, you've got to be kidding me."

Luna and I both shook our heads, but remained silent. Dominick shook his head in disbelief and then looked down at Murray.

"Murray, what's going on here? Are you hurt?"

Murray's eyes fluttered back open, and he smiled in such pure joy when he saw Dominick that my heart twinged for him. Even if he was a jerk, he obviously cared about his friend.

"Dom… you're here. You're dead though. I saw them take your body out. Am I dreaming?" Murray smiled up at him while Dominick gaped at his assistant.

"You're certain I'm dead?" Dominick whispered, clenching his hands into tightly balled fists.

"I... I thought so. Maybe not? The police said you were. I thought they'd killed you, but now I'm not so sure. I don't know what's happening," Murray mumbled.

Dominick whirled on us. "Killed me? I've been murdered? I'm really dead?" Dominick said, his face mottled with shades of red and white as the news began to sink in.

"That's what we're here to help with," Luna said, treading softly. "Can you tell us where you've been or what's happened to you?"

"I don't... I don't know. I've been in this place, I think." Dominick scrubbed his hands over his face. "There's light and nothingness and happiness and everything is just fine. But it feels... in-between. Neither here nor there. Kind of like when you're not awake but you're not fully asleep? That in-between time when you're sort of lucid dreaming," Dominick said.

"I'm sorry," I said to Dominick, surprising him. "You really did die, and we're here to try and put your soul to rest. We want to find who did this to you, but we need your help."

"I... I just need a second," Dominick whispered.

We nodded, happy to give him the time he needed. Not that there's actually an allotted time for coming to terms with these kind of things, but I'm sure I'd need more than a few seconds to adjust to a transition from the corporal realm to the soul world. He looked down at his hands, for the first time seeming to register that he could actually faintly see through them, and held them up to the light. A visible shudder ran through him and I politely looked away, studying some dust catchers on one of my shelves until he spoke again.

"I'm dead."

"Yes. I'm so sorry about that," Luna said. I mean, what else does one say?

"Can you tell me what happened?" Dominick asked softly.

"Your body was found here – in my leopard chair, actually." I pointed to my chair in the corner. "And we know that it was a murder, potentially with poison, but not much else. We need your help because Miss Elva's been taken into custody and we need to get her out."

"A fine woman. We had a great time last night…" Dominick's lips quirked in a smile, then he trailed off at the howl of rage coming from behind the screen to Luna's shop where I presumed Rafe was eavesdropping. The pirate ghost really needed to get over this whole Miss-Elva-and-Dominick thing. It didn't sound like Rafe had been particularly faithful to any one woman during his lifetime, either.

"Do you remember what happened after she left your room?" Luna prompted. Perhaps we could get the information we needed from him instead of having to do the reenactment.

"I remember being very relaxed and quite happy, and then I got a call…" Dominick's mouth snapped shut. He glanced down at Murray with a look of rage, shocking us both, and then he said no more.

"Um, Dominick, we need to ask your permission to do a reenactment spell," Luna said gently.

"What does that do?"

"You agree to let us walk you through the last moments of your life. For you, it will bring closure and understanding. For us, it will solve a mystery and save Miss Elva," Luna said.

Dominick's foot tapped as he thought about it.

"Fine, but I have one requirement," Dominick said.

Luna waved her hand at him to go ahead.

"Murray must be awake enough to watch. He has a very serious lesson to learn."

Chapter Thirty-Two

"YOU REMEMBER what happened to you, don't you?" I asked, wondering if Murray's sadness came from guilt instead of devastation over his friend's death.

"Up to a point. Then things get... foggy," Dominick admitted, and ran a hand over his face before looking sadly at us. "What do you need from me?"

"First, we just need your permission to reenact the events of your death. From my understanding, the spell will lead you through the murder and you'll live through the emotions of it again. It could be quite traumatizing, as we have no idea what happened. Or it could bring you some closure and allow you to move on. But I can't make that decision for you – I can only ask your permission and explain what may happen."

"What would the potential consequences be?" Dominick asked, and I respected him for doing so. You'd think that in death he wouldn't be overly concerned about any sort of backlash on the living world, but it showed that he had been a conscientious practitioner of magick, even if his assistant was off the rails.

"There shouldn't be any consequences in terms of disrupting any negative energy or spirits – the consequences would be more on your end. What if it's revealed that you were betrayed by a family member or something like that? It could add more pain to your passing or make it harder for you to transition," Luna explained.

"I'll be fine," Dominick decided. "I'm not ready to accept that I'm dead, but I'm also strong enough to handle this and do what needs to be done. I'll deal with the emotional backlash of that."

Again, admiration from me for a man I had thought was kind of a jerk. I supposed that would teach me to give people a little more time before making snap judgments. Though in all fairness, he had been super rude just popping into my shop and talking down to me. I'd been right not to like him at the time, but perhaps death was giving him a newfound perspective.

"Then we will run the next spell, which will take a little more time to set up. It will actually lead you through the last moments. For us, it will probably be like watching a movie unfold," Luna said.

"I agree. I'll wait until you're ready. Wake Murray, he must see this," Dominick ordered, and faded back to a corner. I was certain that, now that we'd called him here, he had some personal processing to do, and it was probably best we gave him a few moments of alone time.

"Althea, this is a particularly difficult spell. I'm going to need you to join your power with mine, but due to past…" Luna paused as she sought the right word.

"Screw-ups? Massive disasters?" I supplied sweetly and laughed.

"Discrepancies? Miscalculations?" Luna said, and I gestured for her to continue. "I'll just ask that you find that ball of power in you and visualize blending it with mine. Kind of like two rivers melding together, understood?"

"Got it," I said.

"In the meantime, let's get Murray awake and paying attention," Luna said. She pulled a bottle out of her bag and walked over to him, wafting it under his nose until his eyes fluttered open again. I assumed it was the magickal version of smelling salts.

"Dom," Murray said, looking around, but Dominick stayed hidden in his dark corner – and I assumed he had his own reasons for doing so.

"Yes, that is correct – you did see Dominick," Luna said, watching Murray's eyes for lucidity.

"But how? He's dead," Murray asked.

"He is. But what we are doing in this moment is running a spell that will allow us to see the final moments of his life. Which may be very traumatizing for you. However, Dominick has requested that you be present. It seems he feels you have a very serious life lesson to learn," Luna said, sounding like a schoolteacher lecturing a small child.

Murray's shoulders slumped and he looked down at the floor. "Do I have to? I don't know if I can handle watching this."

"It was his only request. And we needed his permission to run the spell," Luna said.

Murray seemed to shrink within himself until he was

as curled up as he could be, given his restraints. Now I was even more curious what we were about to find out.

"Let's get started," Luna decided, laying out ingredients on my desk. Picking up various bottles of this and that, she added a pinch here, muttered over something else, added a dash from another bottle. Continuing to consult Miss Elva's spell book, she nodded along to herself, confirming each ingredient until she was convinced she had it correct.

Holding the bowl up, she whispered an incantation. There was a flash of light and the ingredients in the bowl turned to a silvery colored dust.

"We're going to spread this along all the edges of the office and outside through the door," Luna explained as she began to sprinkle a line of the silver dust along the wall, over Murray, and continuing around my shop. "Essentially we're enclosing this space to recreate and play for us a moment in time without it disrupting any sort of space-time continuum and not calling forth any other bad energy."

For a moment there, I was completely speechless – which was rare for me. I hadn't even considered that we could be doing something that could interrupt the annals of time. I mean, it wasn't time travel – it was a reenactment.

"I didn't realize this could potentially have such a heavy consequence," I hissed to Luna.

"Big magick can equal big consequences. That's why we take precautions and practice it safely," Luna said.

"Great, just great," I whispered, taking a few deep breaths to calm my growing panic.

"Knock it off. You'll be fine. I just need you to focus

on controlling the flow of your power. Remember, it's soothing, like a river. Hmm, not even like a river – how about like a bubbling brook? Just a trickle of beautiful energy flowing into mine. Focus on that," Luna said. She repeated that to me, her voice soothing and hypnotic, as she wove around the room, distributing her magick dust evenly. When she got to my door she opened it and sprinkled just enough outside to contain the stoop.

"No need to go further out, as I suspect we'll know what we need to know very quickly," Luna decided. "Plus, let's not draw more attention to ourselves than necessary."

Luna joined me back in the circle and checked to make sure Murray was awake and paying attention.

"Ready?" Luna asked me, reaching out to clasp both my hands in hers.

"Ready."

"Light to light, dark to dark, spirits show us the way, let us see the mark," Luna intoned, and then squeezed my hands gently. I took that to mean she wanted me to do the river of energy thing.

Bubbling brook, I reminded myself, and found that white ball of magick within myself. I envisioned it trickling out of me as gently as possible, since my definition of gentle and others' definitions probably varied greatly.

"Good," Luna whispered. "Just keep it kind of flowing in the back of your mind. It's time to step back and watch."

Opening my eyes, I let Luna lead me to the side of the office where Murray sat on the floor, and all three of us waited in silence to see what would happen. Even though I knew we were running one of the biggest magick spells I'd ever been privy to or a part of, it still shocked me when my door opened.

And Dominick stepped in with a gun held to his head.

Chapter Thirty-Three

MURRAY WHIMPERED at my feet and I nudged him so he would keep quiet. It was Dominick's spirit, but he didn't see or acknowledge us. Luna had been right – this was like watching actors in a play work through a scene.

Dominick paused, blocking the view of who held the gun, and refused to move forward.

"I don't understand why you've brought me here," Dominick said.

I jumped. I hadn't expected him to speak, I guess.

Luna squeezed my hand. "Bubbling brook," she whispered, and I realized I needed to keep my energy flowing.

"Because I hate psychics," Cate said, stepping around Dominick and nudging him forward with the gun, keeping his back to her.

Murray let out a gasp, then his shoulders began to shake, silent tears running down his face as he shook his head back and forth. I desperately wanted to know what he knew, but I also wanted to watch what was happening.

"Might I suggest not doing a reality show on psychics,

perhaps?" Dominick said, cool and collected even though his last moments were not far off.

"It'll be my ticket to fame – and redemption," Cate said, her voice steely and the hand holding the gun never faltering. This was not a woman who was acting irrationally or out of passion. She was calm and absolutely in control of the situation; even her hair looked perfect. "I'm going to expose all of you frauds. Blow the whole psychic world to bits and pieces. Such nonsense."

"How does murdering me help with that end goal?" Dominick said.

"It will add intrigue. We've already got reporters interested in the area, psychic phenomena are huge in the media right now, and a murdered psychic is only going to feed the headlines and make a reality show more compelling."

I hated to agree with her, but she was right. The headlines would certainly draw attention.

"Why do you hate psychics?" Dominick asked. Smart man, trying to keep her talking. His eyes darted around the room as he looked for a weapon. What he didn't see was the syringe in her hand. In what looked to be a practiced motion, she reached up and injected him in the neck before he could do anything. Whirling, he went to grab at her but she held the gun with both hands, pointing it at his face.

"You're already dead. Go sit on the chair and we'll have a little chat while the poison works. By my estimate it should be less than five minutes," Cate said.

Dominick closed his eyes, a shudder running through him before he seemed to accept his fate. He moved to my leopard print chair, pulled Herman my skeleton from it, and sat down, the lines of his face set in resignation.

"You see, one day, when I was a child, my dearly departed mother decided to visit a psychic. She was convinced that my father was cheating on her – which I'm sure he wasn't. He was certainly charismatic and enjoyed a good flirt here and there, but I doubt it ever went much further. I was only ten at the time and he was the light of my life. My idol. It was like the sun shone around him," Cate said, sitting back on the edge of the desk and stretching out her legs in front of her. The gun never wavered.

"But this psychic, this madwoman, somehow convinced my mother that my dad was cheating. And she kicked him out! Can you believe that? She said he was a no-good scumbag who only cared about himself. I never saw him after that. Not once. He didn't call, didn't write, didn't try and take me to dinner. He just left. Because of her. And that stupid psychic."

Luna and I glanced at each other, but she just gave a subtle shake to her head. I had about a million and one things I could say about the character of her father and how perhaps her mother had been dead on in her choice to be rid of him, if that was how he treated his daughter.

"Things were never the same after that. My mother tried to compensate for his absence, but I hated her for making my dad leave. She started going to more psychics, getting tarot card readings – she even took a tarot class. Went all deeply spiritual on me and told me the angels or spirit guides would assist me in life if I let them," Cate scoffed. She looked around, her mouth sneering at my altar. "Like there's any such thing as ghosts. I don't believe in any of this crap."

"How will the show make a difference?" Dominick whispered.

"Because my father will see it and know it's me telling him that I forgive him. That I know psychics are just stupid. That none of this is real." Cate gestured around at my shop.

"Why me, though? Why did you choose me to do this to? You could have still accomplished your goal," Dominick said, and I could see the life force starting to drain from him, like the flame of a candle flickering in the wind.

"Your assistant was blackmailing me to try and coerce his way onto the show. I didn't want some of my particularly dirty secrets aired, so I figure this will send him a strong message and drum up more headlines. He didn't believe me when I warned him he'd be sorry for black-mailing me. I believe he will be after this," Cate said, a ruthless smile flitting across her face.

Murray choked on a sob at our feet, a shell of a man being forced to reckon with his actions. I almost felt sorry for him, but I wanted to know just what he had black-mailed Cate with, and what secrets she was still hiding.

"Murray can be overzealous at times, but he isn't a bad person. I'm guessing you did something dreadful for him to want to use it against you," Dominick whispered.

Cate shrugged, not a care in the world. "It's no longer a problem now. Seems to me you're on your way out. Any last words, Dominick?"

"Yes," Dominick said, meeting her gaze dead on. "I'm

a psychic – the real deal – and I can tell you that your father *was* a cheat and a liar. This will all be for nothing. Your mother was right."

With that, he slipped away, the candle blown out.

Cate's face contorted in rage, the first time I'd seen her actually lose control since she'd entered my office. She held the gun in the air and I watched her force herself to calm down, to take a step back, as she'd been about to shoot Dom, my office, and smash everything in sight. Instead, she took a few deep breaths, stood, and calmly assessed the situation. For the first time, I noticed she was wearing gloves. Deftly, Cate raised Dominick's shirt and inscribed voodoo marks on his torso which showed me that Miss Elva, as always, had been right about the marks being fake. Bending to pick up Herman, Cate hummed to herself as she left my office, arranged Herman outside, and walked into the night.

I'd never been witness to such evil before. The level of icy composure necessary to bring herself back from the brink of blind rage – that was a side of crazy I'd never witnessed before.

It was terrifying.

Chapter Thirty-Four

DOMINICK GOT up from the chair, startling me. Then I realized we were now back to just talking with spirit Dominick.

He crouched in front of Murray. "Can you see me?" Dominick asked softly.

Murray nodded, tears streaming down his face. "I'm so sorry," he whispered.

"You couldn't have known it would end like this," Dominick said. "But you have a decision to make – this is one of those life lesson moments, okay?"

"Okay," Murray said, barely able to look at Dom.

"If you want anything in life, you have to work for it. No lying, no going around the back way, and never ever blackmailing. The universe has a way of sorting things out, and this was a very direct and immediate consequence of your blackmail."

Murray's shoulders slumped even lower. "I'm so, so sorry."

"Don't be sorry, just do something about it. You didn't

kill me – Cate did. That's very clear. You don't get to carry the guilt for that, as she's the killer. But something you did to her triggered her actions. You can absolve yourself of that now, if you make it right."

"But how?" Murray asked.

"You need to work with these two here. You've spent too much time going after them when you should have been looking at yourself. Unite for your common goal. And then go forward and be a decent human being. You've got a lot of life to live on this planet. Make me proud."

With that, Dominick just winked out and silence filled the room. Since it seemed like Murray was in a bit of a delicate place at the moment, I resisted the urge to say 'See? I told you so.'

Barely. But you know – that whole adulting thing I was working on.

"Let's close the circle," Luna whispered, deciding to give Murray space to compose himself.

Together Luna and I closed the circle, bringing the magick back in and ending the spell.

As spells went, it had been a cracker. Adrenalin coursed through me and I wanted to rush out and take Cate down or do something, anything, to avenge Dominick. But first we needed to deal with Murray.

Turning, we both leaned back against my desk, crossed our arms and stared down at him. The silence ticked by, then he finally looked up, his eyes as large as a basset hound's as he stared woefully up at us.

"Blackmail, huh?" I asked, getting right into it.

"Yes, I blackmailed Cate. Or tried to," Murray admitted, leaning back against the wall and looking up at the ceiling for a moment.

"What had she done that was worthy of blackmail? And did you want this show so much?" Luna asked, using her charming voice.

Murray paled a bit – if he could get any paler – then whispered something. We both leaned forward.

"What was that?" I asked.

"I said I think she murdered her mother."

Well, shit. I was not expecting that.

"You're telling me you think she murdered her own mother, and instead of just going to the police you *blackmailed* her with it? Did you even consider what could happen if you blackmailed someone who had actually killed before?" I was not using my inside voice, and Luna quickly crossed the room to close and lock the door to my office.

"I couldn't go to the police. It was something I saw in my head – I had an intuition about it. But I had no facts, nothing to give them. You know how the police treat us," Murray said.

I had to concede his point.

"How did her mother die?"

"She'd been battling cancer and died in her sleep. Nothing suspicious about it. But I just had this feeling that it was something more, and so I used it – never thinking it would result in this," Murray said.

"If her mother was already dying, why did she need to kill her?" I wondered out loud.

"To have her say. She was so angry at her mom. It was

her way of being the one to control things to the very end." Murray shrugged.

"She's bat-shit crazy," Luna decided, and we all nodded.

"Murray, this is really bad. We have a lunatic on our hands who's calmly watching us all fall apart so she can film it for a reality show, Miss Elva is in jail, and we have no actual evidence we can give to the police. What are we going to do? Corner her? Force a confession?" I asked.

"I don't know," Murray whispered, still looking like a deflated balloon.

"Murray, did you hear what Dominick said? About changing your life path? Atoning for your actions? What do you want to do moving forward?"

"I... I'll help you both. However you need it. And I'll talk to the police and tell them I blackmailed her. Maybe that will at least get them looking her way," Murray said.

"She may be long gone by the time any of this really comes to light. We need either evidence or a quick confession," Luna said. "But she is intensely scary in a cold and calculating way. You saw how she composed herself. Getting her to break is going to be virtually impossible. She's a brilliant woman."

A thought popped into my head – one so absurd that it might actually work.

"I've got an idea."

Chapter Thirty-Five

REMINDING myself that Miss Elva had made Chief Thomas give us his cell phone number for a reason, I called him as we all piled in the car, a still-shaky Murray slumped in the back seat. He was going to have some tough days ahead as he came to terms with his life choices.

"Althea," Chief Thomas said, "please tell me you aren't doing anything stupid."

"Um, well," I said, "listen, I don't have anything I can give you as evidence. But I'm thinking I can get you a confession if you're there to record it. Or perhaps if I record it?" I said, dodging around his questions because I didn't want to tell him who the killer was.

Here's the thing – I have no problem with police work and doing things by the book. But if he brought Cate in for questioning, she'd dance around it, there would be no evidence, she'd be free to go and then where would we be? Sometimes going around procedure yields better results for everyone.

Which meant I had to keep the chief in the dark for now.

"Why don't you meet me – we'll both have recorders ready – and you be prepared to take someone into custody?" I asked instead.

The silence on the other end of the phone drew out long enough that I looked down to see if I'd dropped the call, then I heard him let out a long breath.

"Miss Elva warned me you were going to pull something like this."

"Warned you! I'm helping her – *and* you," I said, my voice indignant.

"Which she also said." Chief Thomas sighed once more, and I could picture him pinching the bridge of his nose in annoyance.

"Good. So, thoughts?"

"I'll meet you. But if the situation gets out of hand, you need to let me handle it. Do you understand?" Chief Thomas said.

"Um, yes. But, you know, just be a little prepared for the unexpected. Because, well, it's us. Okay, thanks, bye, see you soon," I said, hanging up on Chief Thomas's curses. I looked over at Luna. "He'll meet us. Much to his extreme annoyance with us."

"Murray, you're certain the address is correct?" Luna looked back at Murray.

"Yes, I met her there when I blackmailed her. She's renting the house by the water on the outskirts of town. Not a lot of neighbors, but swanky enough to appeal to her."

We pulled up in the dirt lot down the road from the house and waited for Chief Thomas.

"This is going to be amazing," Rafe said from the backseat, where he was crammed in next to Rosita.

"I'm giving you full permission to be as crazy as you want. But remember the end goal – you want to break her. Send her out screaming, ranting, anything that shakes her to the core so we can get the good stuff."

This could all backfire horribly, I thought, as I drummed my fingers on the wheel. My idea had been farfetched at best, but when the others agreed, I figured it was worth a shot. Maybe, once in a while, I could be the brains behind the operation.

So in all likelihood this was about to fall apart in a fiery disaster.

"Ready to run the spell?"

We all got out of the car and Rosita and Rafe joined hands in front of us, each wearing an excited smile. Luna, Murray, and I joined hands, forming a circle, and we ran a quick spell.

Really, it wasn't a tough one to do. But it would hopefully yield the best results.

When Chief Thomas pulled up, his mouth dropped open.

"Are those... ghosts?" Chief Thomas asked.

"Yes. Can you see them?"

"I see just... kind of wisps of a figure. A woman and a man. A bit of their faces, but nothing too discernable. But, absolutely, yes, I see ghosts." Chief Thomas shivered once, then remembered where he was and who he was with.

"We're sending them in. Let's see if we can break her."

Chapter Thirty-Six

BY LUCK, Cate was sitting on her back porch with a glass of wine, enjoying a cigarette. Tsk, tsk, I thought. That will add lines to your face for the camera.

We'd agreed not to say anything as we drew closer, but I could already see Chief Thomas shaking his head in the dark. I didn't blame him. As crazy went, this was fairly high on the list. But I think the fact that he could actually see ghosts was giving him pause, so he decided to allow this.

Plus, I kind of think he wanted to see what would happen.

We'd told Rafe and Rosita that Cate hated all things supernatural, didn't believe in ghosts, and was a murderer. The goal was for them to terrorize her to the point that she broke and admitted everything. Because if a woman can murder someone as calmly as she did Dominick? She wasn't going to break under interrogation with Chief Thomas. I was certain she'd already thought that conversation through so many times that she'd have all the answers.

We needed to hit her at her weakest point.

Creeping along the side of the house, we found a spot in the shadows, but close enough to the deck that we'd be able to hear anything Cate had to say. Chief Thomas gave me a nod and I looked at a delighted Rafe.

"It's showtime," I whispered, and they both zipped off. Rafe started the assault with a simple swoop-by, causing Cate to glance up from where she scrolled on her phone. Deciding it was nothing, she looked back down.

Rosita floated past behind her, causing Cate's hair to move, and she flinched, looking over her shoulder. Rafe dipped in front of Cate, making her look forward again. Slowly, Cate lowered her phone and looked carefully around.

"Hello?" she called cautiously.

"Hi, beautiful. You know, I've always liked blondes," Rafe said, landing on the table in front of Cate and causing her to jump back, her chair toppling to the floor behind her.

"What... what is this? Is this some joke?" Cate whirled around, but couldn't see us in the cover of darkness.

"I hear you've been a naughty girl, Cate. I like naughty girls," Rafe said, dancing in front of her, his eyes gleaming with delight. I didn't know when he'd last had so much fun. Miss Elva didn't usually allow him to harass the humans.

"Are you a... ghost? A pervert ghost? What is this?" Cate hissed, backing up, her phone clutched in her hand.

"A pervert? How dare you! I was merely admiring your assets," Rafe said, holding a hand to his chest in offense.

I mean, Rafe *was* a pervert ghost, so I couldn't find fault with her assessment.

"I must have fallen asleep," Cate decided, looking around calmly and then nodding briskly to herself. "This is just a dream."

"Oh, it's anything but a dream. We just met your friend Dominick," Rafe said, dropping the hammer.

Cate snapped her head around. "We? Who is we?"

"Me and… your mother," Rafe hissed.

Cate dropped her phone and I winced, hearing the iPhone screen shatter from here. That would be costly to fix, I thought, and then figured she wouldn't much have to worry about that stuff moving forward.

"Mom…" Cate was now turning in a full circle, panic infusing her face.

Rosita floated close, but not too close. We'd kept her blurred enough to show the lines of a woman, but not any discernable features. It was a risk, but we'd hoped it would be enough to drive Cate off the edge.

"You killed me. You ungrateful daughter of mine," Rosita hissed, long and low like we'd instructed her. We figured the more hissing and whispering she did, the better she'd be able to conceal her voice. "You never appreciated all I did for you. How I took care of you after your father abandoned you."

Ouch. Even I winced at that one, and I was the one who'd thought it up. I didn't know if Cate was capable of feeling guilt, so I had gone with my gut instinct – because I knew for certain she was capable of rage.

"Daddy didn't abandon me," Cate said, stalking forward until she stood close to where Rosita hovered. The ghost had been smart, leading her closer to us, and her words were clear as day for our recorders. "He loved me."

"He loved chasing after women more. Why do you think he never came to see you?"

"Because of you!" Cate shrieked. "You kept him away. I know he wouldn't just walk away from me like that. You weren't woman enough for him."

Rosita reared back, flitting in violent circles around Cate, causing the woman to spin.

"I was more than enough woman for him. He was a weak man who constantly needed attention – his ego and other parts stroked incessantly. I was right to kick him out. You never wanted to see that," Rosita said. I was astounded at how well she was embracing this role.

"I was right to kill you," Cate screeched.

Chief Thomas closed his eyes for a moment, already reaching for his cuffs.

"Killing is never the answer," Rosita said. "Yet you did it again. Did you really think killing Dominick would bring your father back?"

Cate's eyes were wild, and I could see her cracking, as sure as if she were glass shattering on the ground.

"His little shit assistant was blackmailing me about your inconsequential death. You were going to die anyway, who cares that I helped it along? At least you knew how much I hated you for taking my father from me," Cate hissed, stalking forward. She was now actively chasing Rosita around the deck, and the ghost darted every which way. "I enjoyed getting rid of Dominick. The headlines are already amazing – my boss called and wants me to do a documentary now – and you silly woman, you can't stop me. My father's going to see my name in lights!"

"That'll never happen, sweetie," Rosita said, her voice both mean and sad at the same time.

Cate whirled when she heard footsteps. Chief Thomas had stepped onto the deck.

"You have the right to remain silent..."

"No," Cate shrieked. "No, I will not go down for this! I have a plan – a future! You hear me? None of you in this crazy little town with its stupid little psychics are going to take me down. I don't believe you or any of this. It's all a lie!"

She lunged for her purse, where I'm sure her gun was, but Rafe intercepted in what I could only say was a feat of brilliance. He let her rush right through him, which I knew from past experience felt like cruising through ice. She froze for an instant, the last wheels of sanity rolling away in her brain.

Chief Thomas caught her and cuffed her, her rambles nothing but lunacy as tears streaked her pretty cheeks. Looking at me, he mimicked zipping his lips. I knew he still had to keep his recorder on all the way back to the station. We'd discussed this beforehand and had agreed we wanted no record of us being there.

Easing our way back, we slipped away in the darkness, making it to my car and driving sedately away as though nothing had just happened. It wasn't until we were a good five minutes away that I let out a cheer.

"For once! I had a good idea!"

Okay, okay, maybe the adulting thing still needed some work.

Epilogue

I WAS SO excited I felt like jumping up and down. Finally, Beau's new restaurant was opening, and I could gush over all the amazing finishing touches and taste the food he'd poured his heart and soul into. I'd even bought myself a new dress for the occasion.

"You look amazing," Trace said with a whistle when I came downstairs. I'd chosen fire-engine red, with a nice dip to show my cleavage, and a skirt that ended just below my knees. I'd deepened my teal hair color to an almost midnight blue and my eyes popped with the new smoky shadow I'd bought. I felt like a million bucks, and told Trace as much.

"And you don't look so bad yourself," I said, wrapping my arms around him. It was too warm for suit coats here, but he had a nice white linen shirt on, and pressed khakis. His hair was suitably tamed and his tan popped against his shirt. Turning us, he stood so we looked in the mirror at ourselves as a couple.

"We look good together, Thea," Trace said, his breath warm against my ear.

I shivered as goosebumps ran down my neck. "We do. I like us," I admitted.

"Then let's keep us rocking," Trace said, and kissed me once more before whistling to let Hank out the back before we had to leave.

My plan had worked out beautifully, if I do say so myself. The recording had held up, but even if it hadn't, Cate was an open book in interrogation. It was like she'd kept a wall up her whole life, never letting the emotions out, and once she'd cracked – she'd cracked. Everything came pouring out and Chief Thomas had an open-and-closed case in a matter of hours.

Miss Elva had actually enjoyed her time in jail, if you can believe that. It had given her some stimulation, let her meet some other jailbirds with fascinating stories, and now she got to say things like, "Well, when I was in prison" if she needed to shut someone up at a dinner party.

The most surprising had been Murray. He'd confessed everything to Chief Thomas, who in turn had decided that – since he had readily admitted his crime, had worked to help find the killer, and was deeply apologetic and missing his friend – Murray would be let go with a slap on the wrist. Instead of leaving town immediately, Murray had asked if he could stay. Not only did he feel bad for what he'd done, but he decided he wanted to go into something more peaceful. He'd taken a job as a crew member on a yacht and was going to work toward getting his captain's license. On the side, he'd started working with a program that taught troubled youth how to sail and work the trades.

All in all, I had to say I thought Dominick would have been proud.

Arriving at Beau's new high-end seafood restaurant a little while later, I was delighted to see his soft opening already full of people. Candles lined the sidewalk outside and fairy lights twinkled around the windows. Trace and I eased inside and my eyes darted around the room until I could find Beau. Spotting him across the room, I slipped away from Trace, who was speaking to a client. I made a beeline for Beau and squeezed him in a huge hug.

"This place is amazing! I'm so proud of you. A million times over. You've made Lucky's a screaming success, and you'll do the same here. I'm proud to call you my best friend," I gushed, over-the-moon excited for him. He looked extra handsome tonight in a crisp button-down shirt with little anchors embroidered on the cuffs, and a smile a mile wide on his face.

"Isn't it great? Look at your photo too," Beau gushed, pointing to where he'd blown up a black and white underwater photograph I'd taken. It was a turtle, seemingly giving the camera a cheeky grin, and it looked extra edgy and artsy since it was shot in black and white. Beneath it, the tables with their cheerful flowers, subdued linens, and beautiful candles looked fun, artsy, and elegant all at once.

"It looks great, and I'm not just saying that because I have to," I laughed, hugging him again. "You've hit just the right touch with everything here. It's amazing."

"I have to work the room. Plan to stay late, okay? We'll split a bottle of wine and talk about all the gossip," Beau said, already being pulled away to answer some questions for the local newspaper.

"Althea."

I froze before pasting a smile on my face and turning.

"Cash, I wasn't expecting you'd be here," I said.

"I couldn't miss out on Beau's big night," Cash said, his grey eyes shrewd in his face as he examined me. He looked as handsome as ever, his shirt fitting muscled arms perfectly, not a hair out of place on his head. Lightly tanned, and with the gloss that only the magnificently rich carried, he would always cause me to catch my breath. "This is Hannah, by the way. Hannah, meet Althea."

I smiled brightly at the woman draped on his arm, though I kind of wanted to smash some food in her face. Tiny – as in, barely five foot two – with a miniscule waist, a fitted Gucci dress, and miles of straight blonde hair, she looked just as polished and glistening as Cash did. They were a perfect match. So why did looking at them make my heart hurt?

"Nice to meet you. What a beautiful place – I'm excited to try the food," Hannah said. I smiled and said something nonsensical back. Of course she had to be nice too.

An arm wrapped around my waist and I immediately felt calmer for having Trace by my side.

"Cash." Trace nodded at him, barely concealing a glare.

"Trace, always a pleasure," Cash said, his lips quirking in a smile that almost had me smiling back. These two had quite the history when it came to me.

"We're off to sample some of the food stations. I just wanted to say a quick hello. Stay out of trouble, Althea. And take care of her, Trace," Cash said. And with that, he was gone, seeming to take some of the energy with him as he went.

My eyes followed him across the room, and a teeny tiny part of me wondered – what if?

"That guy," Trace said, scowling into my ear.

I turned, laughing up at him. "Buy me a drink, handsome? I know of this boat where we can sneak away to…"

Trace's eyes lit up and he brushed a kiss over my lips.

"I like the sound of that."

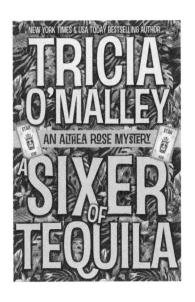

Available as an e-book, paperback or audiobook!
Available from Amazon

The following is an excerpt from A Sixer of Tequila

Book 6 in the Althea Rose Mystery Series

Chapter One

"THE FLAMINGO'S BEEN STOLEN."

I leaned back on my stool and unabashedly eavesdropped on the women gossiping next to me under the thatched roof of Lucky's Tiki Bar, run by my best friend Beau. He winked at me from where he was building a mai-tai in one of the tiki mugs from his new custom line of mugs – this one in a shark shape – and I knew he was listening in as well.

"Can you believe it? Who would steal a six-foot-tall flamingo?" Woman number one, in a floral dress and tasteful flats, shook her head sadly as if to say *What is the world coming to?*

I, too, wondered what this world was coming to, but more because I was concerned over the taste of someone who would actually order a six-foot-tall flamingo. Granted, I shouldn't be passing judgment on other people's design tastes, as mine ran to the decidedly more eclectic side of things.

"They say it was going to be at the entrance for the

new mini-golf course. They were going to unveil it and surprise the town this week." Woman number two, dark circles under her eyes and hair in an unkempt ponytail, shrugged. "Which is too bad. I've been telling the kids I had a surprise for them. At the very least, it would have been something to wear off some of their incessant energy."

That explained the dark circles and messy hair, I thought, and sipped delicately on my mojito as I considered the news. Tuning them out as they began to discuss their kids – a topic that could often send me straight to sleep – I wondered what had happened to the flamingo.

"Think it's just teens having a prank?" Beau came and leaned forward on the bar, his golden good looks and air of confidence making both men and women alike fall for him on the regular. But he only played for one team – and too bad it wasn't mine, I thought, once again admiring his handsome face and easy surfer style.

"Doesn't feel that way to me," I said. "But I also didn't know we were getting a mini golf course, so there's that."

"Didn't you? It's been the talk of the town for weeks now," Beau said with a smile. "Everyone's complaining about the name."

"No! I hadn't heard," I admitted, leaning closer. "Is it bad?"

"Flocking Flamazing Mini-Golf," Beau said, his eyes crinkling at the corners as he did his best not to laugh.

"Shut up. That's amazing," I breathed, immediately wondering what the Whittiers, Tequila Key's upper-crust family, would have to say about that. Frankly, I was surprised Theodore Whittier hadn't stopped the development in its tracks already. He was on the board of everything in town, as he liked to tell anyone who cared to listen.

I never did.

"Don't you mean *fla*-mazing?" Beau asked. I laughed out loud this time while Beau went off to serve some tourists who had just arrived at the end of the bar.

Tequila Key was just a bump on the road on the way to the party town of Key West. I liked the sleepiness of the town, where everyone knew everyone and something as small as a new mini-golf course was enough to send the town into full gossip mode. Years ago, some intrepid mayor had decided to put a sign on the highway proclaiming, "Tequila Makes it Better," thus ensuring that no tourists would ever actually visit Tequila Key. Instead they just stopped to take a ridiculous selfie by the sign before continuing on their way. I was more than happy with this arrangement, though I'd heard murmurs lately about a new town campaign seeking to encourage more tourism. Personally, after the last few months I'd had, more tourists were the last thing I was looking for. My name had been splashed across the tabloids more than once, and I was finally settling back into a normal routine with nobody hounding me for psychic information.

Aside from my clients, that is.

I'm Althea Rose, co-owner of the Luna Rose Potions & Tarot Shop. I was recently outed to the world as a psychic by several gossip magazines and a reality show producer – whom I'd subsequently helped put in jail – and my client list has exploded ever since. Granted, I shouldn't say I'd been 'outed' – I'd never hidden the fact of who or what I was – but I certainly didn't enjoy looking at my life through the lens of a tabloid magazine. Not to mention that the editors liked to choose the most unflattering photos of me they could find. It was enough to put anyone off wearing a swimsuit in public ever again.

"Did you hear about the flamingo?" Luna, my other best friend and colleague, slid onto a stool next to me, looking imminently cool and perfectly put-together in her white linen maxi-dress, not a wrinkle in sight. I mean, how was that even fair? Not only was she coolly gorgeous with flowing blond hair, twinkling blue eyes, and a smile that could drop men to their knees, but even her linen dresses didn't crease. I suspected, as I had on more than one occasion, that she used a glamour spell to keep her whites white and her clothes unwrinkled.

There were some extra benefits to being a white witch, I supposed.

"Apparently that's the gossip of the hour," I said. I nodded to the two women who were walking out the door, presumably to attend to their aforementioned children, and turned to look back at Luna. "How did I not even know there's going to be a mini-golf course going in?"

"You've been pretty tied up. Between the deluge in clients and your new love life, I'm surprised you've even had time to come up for air," Luna said, nodding to Beau when he held up a bottle of pinot grigio.

"It's not a love life," I protested, squirming in my seat.

"Fine, sex life. Whatever you want to call it." Luna blew out an exasperated breath – well, as close to exasperated as she gets with me – and gratefully accepted the glass of wine Beau handed her.

"Oh, are we talking about sex? Whose sex life?" Beau said, leaning in, his eyes dancing in curiosity.

"Althea's." Luna gestured to me with her wine glass. "I'm just pointing out that she's doing the thing she always does when she first starts dating someone and disappears off the radar for a while. Which is how she didn't know about the mini-golf course, let alone the stolen flamingo."

"Well, in all fairness, the flamingo bit is a new twist," Beau said, ever my champion. "But yeah, she's totally doing her hermit thing. We're just her friends when she's not having sex."

So much for being my champion.

"That's not true!" I tugged a lock of my hair, dyed blue this month, and glared at them. "You all know how nutso my life was after the tabloids. I could barely go outside after we were involved with that reality show producer. And, well, yes, I like sex. So sue me. It's good stress relief."

"You'd think she'd be less bitchy with all the sex she's getting," Luna pointed out.

"Right? Like, where is the relaxed Althea we all know and love?"

"I'm right here," I pouted as I took another sip of my mojito.

"See? That's the face you'd think she wouldn't be making after all the sex she's having."

"I'm not cranky," I insisted. "I just don't like you insinuating that I drop my friends as soon as I'm dating someone."

"You don't drop us, you just take a small holiday,"

Luna amended, carefully brushing away a small speck of dust on the bar that had dared to get close to her dress.

"Doesn't everyone, though? I seem to remember you disappearing for a significant amount of time once you and Mathias hooked up." Luna had the decency to look away and hum. "And you, Beau – I know the minute you're hooking up because you start buying new clothes."

"Date outfits," Beau agreed.

"Well? I'm here, aren't I? When I could be home shagging a sexy dive instructor. So can we all appreciate that?"

"Appreciated." Luna ran her hand gently down my arm. "Now, who would steal a six-foot flamingo?"

"And why do I feel like you're about to get involved in it?" Beau said, glaring at me.

"Me?" I squeaked, pointing a finger at my chest. "I don't care about this stupid flamingo."

"But you love a mystery." Luna tucked a wisp of blonde hair behind her ear. "I don't have a great feeling about this, I'll be honest."

"It's just a flamingo. What harm could come from finding out who took a silly plastic statue? As Beau said, it's probably just teens playing a prank."

"I don't like flamingos," Luna said.

I gaped at her. "How can you not like flamingos? They're like…" I stopped, considering my words.

"The Beaus of the bird world? Though I think I'd prefer parrots, but parrots squawk way more than I do."

Both Luna and I suddenly found other things to look at in the restaurant.

"Ohhhh… aren't we both being bitchy today? I see how it is. Just for that, I'm going to make you a flamazing flamingle martini and you're going to love every drop of it."

"Flamingle?" Luna wondered out loud to Beau's retreating back.

"Trust me, you'll flocking love it."

Available from Amazon

Afterword

Thank you for spending time with my book, I hope you enjoyed the story.

Have you read books from my other series? Join our little community by signing up for my newsletter for updates on island-living, giveaways, and how to follow me on social media!
http://eepurl.com/1LAiz.

or at my website
www.triciaomalley.com

Please consider leaving a review! Your review helps others to take a chance on my stories. I really appreciate your help!

Finding happiness is the best revenge

New from Tricia O'Malley - Ms. Bitch
Read Today

From the outside, it seems thirty-six-year-old Tess Campbell has it all. A happy marriage, a successful career as a novelist, and an exciting cross-country move ahead. Tess has always played by the rules and it seems like life is good. Except it's not. Life is a bitch. And suddenly so is Tess.

"Ms. Bitch is sunshine in a book! An uplifting story of fighting your way through heartbreak and making your own version of happily-ever-after."

~Ann Charles, USA Today Bestselling Author of the Deadwood Mystery Series

"Authentic and relatable, Ms. Bitch packs an emotional punch. By the end, I was crying happy tears and ready to pack my bags in search of my best life."

-Annabel Chase, author of the Starry Hollow Witches series

"It's easy to be brave when you have a lot of support in your life, but it takes a special kind of courage to forge a new path when you're alone. Tess is the heroine I hope I'll be if my life ever crumbles down around me. Ms. Bitch is a journey of determination, a study in self-love, and a hope for second chances. I could not put it down!"

-Renee George, USA Today Bestselling Author of the Nora Black Midlife Psychic Mysteries

"I don't know where to start listing all the reasons why you should read this book. It's empowering. It's fierce. It's about loving yourself enough to build the life you want. It was honest, and raw, and real and I just...loved it so much!"

– Sara Wylde, author of Fat

The Althea Rose Series

ALSO BY TRICIA O'MALLEY

One Tequila

Tequila for Two

Tequila Will Kill Ya (Novella)

Three Tequilas

Tequila Shots & Valentine Knots (Novella)

Tequila Four

A Fifth of Tequila

A Sixer of Tequila

Seven Deadly Tequilas

Available in audio, e-book & paperback!

Available from Amazon

"Not my usual genre but couldn't resist the Florida Keys setting. I was hooked from the first page. A fun read with just the right amount of crazy! Will definitely follow this series."- Amazon Review

The Isle of Destiny Series

ALSO BY TRICIA O'MALLEY

Stone Song

Sword Song

Spear Song

Sphere Song

Available in audio, e-book & paperback!

Available from Amazon

"Love this series. I will read this multiple times. Keeps you on the edge of your seat. It has action, excitement and romance all in one series."- Amazon Review

The Siren Island Series

ALSO BY TRICIA O'MALLEY

Good Girl

Up to No Good

A Good Chance

Good Moon Rising

Too Good to Be True

Available in audio, e-book & paperback!

Available from Amazon

"Love her books and was excited for a totally new and different one! Once again, she did NOT disappoint! Magical in multiple ways and on multiple levels. Her writing style, while similar to that of Nora Roberts, kicks it up a notch!! I want to visit that island, stay in the B&B and meet the gals who run it! The characters are THAT real!!!" - Amazon Review

Author's Note

Thank you for taking a chance on my books; it means the world to me. Writing novels came by way of a tragedy that turned into something beautiful and larger than itself (see: *The Stolen Dog*). Since that time, I've changed my career, put it all on the line, and followed my heart.

Thank you for taking part in the worlds I have created; I hope you enjoy it.

I would be honored if you left a review online. It helps other readers to take a chance on my work.

As always, you can reach me at info@triciaomalley.com or feel free to visit my website at www.triciaomalley.com.

Author's Acknowledgement

First, and foremost, I'd like to thank my family and friends for their constant support, advice, and ideas. You've all proven to make a difference on my path. And, to my beta readers, I love you for all of your support and fascinating feedback!

And last, but never least, my two constant companions as I struggle through words on my computer each day - Briggs and Blue.

Made in the USA
Las Vegas, NV
23 May 2024

90295718R00142